DEAD MEN
DO
TELL TALES

BY WESLEY MARKS

ISBN-10: 0-9992673-10
ISBN-13: 978-0-9992673-18

Published by TTT publications

Book layout by www.ebooklaunch.com

Acknowledgments

It is always exciting and terrifying writing your first book to publish, because all you can think about as you pour out your story is you hope someone will read it and like it. I think I experienced those emotions every time I sat down at the computer to write. Luckily, I have had a small group of people who have helped me to complete this project. Let me begin with my two daughters, Alicia Marks and Lauren Marks Gao, who proofread for me, making suggestions and trying to clarify those places where my fingers couldn't translate my thoughts. You two are always on my mind and in my heart, and as a father I am pleased with how you have turned out despite me being your father.

To the wonderful librarian at the school where I teach, Jennifer Hashert, who took the time to read through and do the initial edits of my manuscript. I also had three of my students who took their winter break to read the book and leave me suggestions not just on the script but also helped make sure the book cover was engaging to readers their age. Thank you, Aimee Beltran, Alexa Gonzalez, and Jackeline Vasquez for reading and participating with me. My hope is that all three of you young ladies will grow up to be the wonderful women that I see in you. In all fairness, you did get out of a major assessment for your trouble, but none of you would have struggled with it anyway.

Finally, a huge thank-you to the woman who helped me create the final product, which was better than I could have imagined, Joan Giurdanella. I was completely horrified by what she did to my manuscript. I have students who talk about how harshly I edit and mark up their papers, but that does not compare to what Joan did to mine. She had me questioning my skills at first, but then I saw what she was doing and why. She corrected, butchered, and hacked up the text much like vegetables going into a gumbo, but the end result was more than I could have expected, and for that she receives all of my praise.

—Wesley Marks
July 2017

Chapter 1

The Storm, July 4, 1502

"We should have taken Columbus's advice about the weather," screamed Antonio de Torres over the ferocious sound of the waves and wind. He realized that his flotilla was in peril. But Governor Francisco de Bobadilla did not want to hear it. Columbus was a criminal in his eyes. Just two years prior, he had Columbus and his brothers arrested for abusing their power governing Hispaniola, but the king and queen had freed them. That bitterness blinded Bobadilla's reasoning, and his decision to have the fleet leave Santo Domingo with him aboard now placed thirty-two ships, six hundred men, and the king and queen's largest treasure in the vengeful arms of what would prove to be the worst hurricane imaginable.

Storms were nothing new to Captain de Torres; he had encountered hundreds in his thirty years of sailing. His handpicked crews and their experienced captains, including his only son, Franco, knew their trade. They would do their best to fight through this storm—they had to—because the cargo was too precious and the lives of his men priceless. But he had to wonder: Had he used poor judgment this time? Had the governor's pressure influenced him into taking an unnecessary risk?

In each flash of lightning, Antonio de Torres strained to see any of the caravels that had left port under his command. In total, thirty-two ships had sailed from Santo Domingo bound for Spain with *El Dorado* as the fleet's flagship. Now it seemed they were all trapped between hurricane-force winds and waves that seemed tall enough to swallow them whole, feasting on thousands of tons of gold meant for the Spanish crown and washing it down with lives of the crew. With each flash, Antonio could see fewer and fewer ships. Perhaps they were being bashed to pieces by the nearby reefs or pushed farther and farther off course by the waves and wind.

His valiant sailors had triple-reefed the sails to expose as little cloth as possible to the storm and still give them some control. They stayed at their posts lashed to the guy lines to keep from being swept overboard with every angry wave. But as hard as they tried, staying afloat proved to be an almost impossible task. This beast of a storm continued to bat around the ninety-foot *El Dorado*, and the merciless pounding began to take its toll. First the mizzenmast snapped like a twig underfoot, crushing two crewmen as they dove for safety. Then the rest of the rigging broke loose whipping across the deck like a dragon's tail, scraping away everything and everyone who got in its path. Next came the crashing sound of the main mast buckling under the pressure of the wind. Finally, the rudder, the last hope of human control, was ripped from the brackets that held it in place. Mastless, rudderless, and almost crewless, *El Dorado* was at the mercy of Poseidon.

Antonio de Torres knew that the end was near. His flagship was still afloat. But with no control and most of her crew lost to the sea, there were only a few options. He and Governor Bobadilla could abandon ship in a long boat that most likely would not last more than a few minutes in these seas, or he could wait for *El Dorado* to gasp her last breath and slip to the abyss below. There was no hope for him or the gold, which he would have gladly traded for his life. Bobadilla chose the long boat, filling it with provisions and waited for the next wave to carry him away to safety. Instead, the wave hurled him out to sea like an angry baby throwing his rattle out of his crib. The impact collapsed the long boat, and the sea swallowed up Bobadilla and its remains much like Jonah and the whale. Now alone, the captain waited aboard *El Dorado*.

The solitude brought the thoughts of his life passing before him as each angry wave rushed by. He remembered his childhood on the coast of Spain, watching the valiant brave seamen leave their families and head out to their mistress, the open sea, and dreaming of the day when he, too, would take his place among the valiant men he adored. He recalled his first captain, harsh but fair, and the things he learned as he grew the skills to take command of his own ship. He thought of the love of his life, the woman he had met soon after becoming captain, and the three beautiful children she gave him. Finally, Antonio called to mind Franco, his son, who like him was in peril and whom he could no longer see on the horizon. If he had just encouraged his son to be a merchant or shopkeeper, Franco's life would be safe now.

El Dorado spun and twisted with no rudder and bounced and bucked with each wave driving the ship farther away from its original course. Passing through the Mona Passage, but not knowing it, the ship remained afloat with no distinct direction. *El Dorado* was at the mercy of the hurricane. Any other ship would have been swamped by the sheer size of the waves. Fortunately, the well-built flagship contained enough added ballast—the treasure—that she seemed to roll with each punch and then right herself ready to take another. She continued being battered and tossed for several days. The storm's constant barrage finally took its toll as the ship began listing to one side. Water easily began to find its way into the cargo hold. Preparing for the worst, Captain Antonio de Torres made a last entry in his log then wrapped it in oilcloth and sealed it in a barrel. Tying a rope around his waist, he lashed himself to the barrel and waited for the end. He hoped that the barrel would save him or that a passing ship would find his body. He waited through the night until the wave with his name on it finally came and swept him off the deck. Flung through the air, he smashed into an outcropping of rocks. Life slipped slowly away from his mangled body as the wind and waves carried away the hulk of his ship. He did not know that he would die within a few strokes of land. His remains were washed up onto the tan sands on the shore, and the ship was transported in the darkness of the night to an unknown grave.

Four captains, including Franco de Torres, survived the horrendous hurricane, washing up on an island miles away from their port of debarkation and hundreds of miles from the final resting place of *El Dorado*. Though Franco searched for his father's remains and the broken hull of *El Dorado*, he went to his grave not knowing his father's fate.

Chapter 2

Present-Day Dallas, Texas

"Every summer is the same. I go with Dad as he searches for a silly snail he is studying!" exclaimed Dalton to his friend Juan at the end of soccer practice in late April.

Being the son of a malacologist was boring. Every summer, Dalton Miller and his father, Dr. Frank Miller, tramped off to some pond to look at snails. Rarely did Dalton's mother, Linda, go hunting snails; she preferred eating escargot rather than picking them up out of the mud. As soon as Dalton got out of school, he and Dr. Miller would go off to some part of America where there was another slimy little creature to be studied. Most of the time, Dalton just sat and played video games on his DSI unless his father dragged him out in rubber waders to hold a can or dip some mucky water. This year, they were scheduled to go to Florida, but not Disney World or Universal Studios, but a marsh outside of Naples. Surprisingly, Dr. Miller said that Dalton could take a friend to keep me company.

Dalton, excited about the prospect of taking someone with him to keep his summer from being so boring, asked his closest friend, Juan, to join him, as long as his parents approved.

Juan Hernandez was Dalton's best friend in Texas. Dr. Miller had moved his family to Dallas four years ago from Des Moines, Iowa. He had received a grant to teach biology and research snail reproduction at Southern Methodist University, so Dallas became Dalton's new home. Although his family moved every few years, Dalton still found it difficult even if he was friendly and intelligent. Always being the new guy or the tall lanky kid, he struggled to fit in unless he had a chance to join a soccer team. Most would have thought basketball because of his height. But Dalton loved soccer from the time he was a little kid watching it being played on the college campuses where his father worked. There was something magical about the fluid movements and viciousness about attacking the prey at the other end of the pitch. He even plastered his bedroom with posters of great players and beautiful stadiums.

The realtor, who helped the Millers find a house in Dallas, noticed Dalton's soccer shirt and mentioned she had a son who played, so she introduced Dalton to the team. The first day of soccer practice, Dalton collided with a small, fast midfielder named Juan Hernandez. Picking themselves up off of the grass, everyone thought there would be trouble between the new, tall white kid and the feisty Latino boy.

Instead, Dalton reached down, extended his hand, and said, "That was some move you just put on me. I thought I'd get it by you, but that didn't work. Sometime you are going to have to show me how you did it. My name is Dalton."

Laughing, the good-natured Juan took Dalton's hand to get to his feet and responded, "I'm Juan. You must be the guy Ted's mom was talking about."

From that moment, they became inseparable. They made a strange pair of fourteen-year-olds, Dalton already pushing six feet with his sandy blond hair and long legs, and Juan barely stretching to five feet three with a dark complexion and a ferocious smile. Rarely, did you see one without the other. They would sit at lunch talking about soccer and girls, and then after school and practice they could be found in front of a gaming console battling it out for hours. So, it was a given that Dalton would invite Juan to go with him for the summer.

The excitement of a potential summer of hanging out with each other in a strange place was almost uncontainable. As soon as the last soccer drill was over and the equipment put away, the boys ran to Mrs. Hernandez's car to ask about going. Juan flung open the car door and jumped inside and began nearly screaming in Spanish, as he often did when he was excited, to his mother. He was talking so fast that she had to slow him down so she could understand him. As Juan still spoke in a fast high-pitch tone gesturing so wildly with his hands Dalton thought his best friend might just take off flying.

"Can I go to Florida with Dalton for the summer?" Juan finally blurted out in English.

"What?" his mother asked.

"Dalton's father is going to Florida to study snails this summer, and he told Dalton he could invite me to go. Can I?" asked Juan.

Mrs. Hernandez answered with a lot of questions: "What would you and Dalton do? Where would you stay?"

Over the course of the year, the two families had gotten to know each other pretty well through soccer games and practices and even dinners together. Unbeknownst to the boys, Dr. Miller had already spoken with Juan's parents. Mrs. Hernandez had already made her decision without letting the boys know she was aware of the trip.

"We will have to talk to your father about this," she said. "He may have already made plans for you, Juan."

Dalton and Juan begged persistently all twenty blocks home in the car as she just smiled at them in the rearview mirror.

When they arrived at Juan's home, the boys waited impatiently for Juan's father to get back from work. In the meantime, they planned, schemed, and dreamed about the adventures they would have: playing video games all night, eating junk food, and even wrestling alligators in the swamp. With the imagination of two fourteen-year-old boys, the sky was the limit for these two balls of energy. Every few minutes, they peeked out the window checking the drive anxiously for Mr. Hernandez's arrival. To them, it seemed worse than taking a math test in Ms. Jones's class. Never in their lives had they felt an hour seem like a lifetime. When the blue Chevy pickup pulled in the driveway, they burst through the front door clearing the porch and steps like gazelles. They were standing at the truck's door before Juan's father could release his seat belt, jumping around as if they were standing in a fire ant bed. Their chatter was so fast and incoherent that Mr. Hernandez had to honk the horn to make them stop.

"What's going on? Is the house on fire or has Mom been kidnapped by aliens?" Juan's father cried.

Juan starting talking so fast that Mr. Hernandez had to reach out and put his hand over Juan's mouth to stop him.

"Slow down and tell me what's going on," his father huffed.

Juan slowed down and told him all about Dr. Miller's trip to Florida and the fact that he had been invited to go with Dalton to keep him company for the summer.

"Can I go with them?" Juan finally blurted out.

"Let me talk to your mother first, and then we will make a decision," answered his father walking toward the house but secretly knowing his decision.

It was as if time stood still while Juan's parents talked and questioned Dalton. They wanted to know everything about the trip, where they going, how long they would stay, and what they would be doing. With each question, the boys' frustration grew. They thought the answer would be no. After what seemed like a century, Juan's parents finally made a decision.

"You may go with Dalton and Dr. Miller and spend the summer in Florida hunting snails," Mr. and Mrs. Hernandez said in unison.

The boys could not contain their excitement. Jumping to his feet, Juan hugged his mother and father and then he and Dalton ran into Juan's bedroom jabbering like magpies. Immediately, they got on the

Internet to research things to do in Florida. The boys Googled Naples, Florida, to see what it looked like and what was around. They found out it was on the edge of the Everglades because that was where Dalton's father was going to do his research. Besides the swamp, the Gulf of Mexico with its white beaches was close by, so they could chase alligators or sharks if they felt adventurous.

When Mrs. Miller came to pick up Dalton, the boys told her the news. The next four weeks of school proved to be torturous for them knowing that a summer of excitement waited for them. If they had only known how Mr. Bagwell's American history class would come in handy, they would not have acted so bored in it.

Chapter 3

The Road Trip

The night before Dr. Miller, Dalton, and Juan were set to leave, they packed the green Jeep Grand Cherokee with luggage, sample cases, nets, and rubber waders, allowing only enough room for the three of them. A two-wheeled trailer carried a small boat behind the Jeep. The sun had not yet risen, but getting the two boys up during their summer vacation was not a problem. As soon as Mrs. Miller walked into Dalton's room and turned on the lights, her son and Juan got dressed and headed to the car.

The real trouble had been getting them to sleep the night before. Juan had spent the night so that they could get on the road early, but that did not mean the boys went to sleep at a reasonable time. They were as wound up as a year clock, the kind that doesn't use batteries but requires you to turn a key to tighten the spring. Three times Dalton's mother had to go into the bedroom to quiet the boys down because Dr. Miller had to sleep so he would be rested for the long drive.

The early hour and the dark put the boys back to sleep before they left Dallas. The traffic that morning was light with only eighteen-wheelers headed to their unknown destinations east on Interstate 20 toward Shreveport, Louisiana. By the time they reached Longview, Texas, the boys were stirring and "dying from hunger." Knowing that if he didn't stop he would have a mutiny on his hands, Dr. Miller pulled over at a McDonald's, and the boys devoured their pancakes and sausage as if they had not eaten in years.

"We can go two different ways to get to Naples, one through Montgomery, Alabama, and then south, or through New Orleans and then stay along the coast. What would be your choice?" inquired Dr. Miller.

It did not make any difference to him, so he allowed the boys to choose since it was also their vacation. The boys in unison blurted out New Orleans. Neither one had ever been there, and remembering their American history teacher, Mr. Bagwell, talk about New Orleans made them anxious to see this slice of history. The great stories of pirates and the French and even its place in the Civil War had their imaginations running wild about this city, which was home to Mardi Gras.

Just inside of Shreveport, Louisiana, Dr. Miller took the loop around the city, turned south on Interstate 49 cutting through Alexandria, Louisiana, and then turned east again on Interstate 10 at Lafayette. As the car drew closer to New Orleans, the boys could see the swamp on both sides of the road. Neither had ever seen an alligator in the wild, so they pressed their faces against the windows and peered out into the bayous. It became a game to see who could see an alligator, but moving seventy miles an hour on a paved road made it almost impossible. They saw cypress trees, brackish water, egrets, and even a possum, but no alligators. Mile after mile, the swamp kept going until finally they began to get closer to the city.

When Dr. Miller and the boys arrived in the Big Easy, they spent the night at a hotel just off of Canal Street in the French Quarter. What better way to teach the boys about history than to let them spend a day experiencing this almost three-hundred-year-old city. The boys walked in Jackson Square with all of the artists, fortune-tellers, musicians, and jugglers. Then they walked the streets lined with voodoo shops, spice stores touting the hottest hot sauce, and cafés and restaurants emitting aromas conjuring up their signature food dishes. They rode the streetcars, which run up and down many streets, seeing magnificent old houses, shops, and even cemeteries with their above-ground tombs.

Going to New Orleans would not be complete without eating Cajun food like étouffée, a crawfish and rice dish with a spicy sauce. Who would have ever thought the critters caught in drainage ditches that looked like little lobsters could be so tasty?

Even with all of the delicious smells, loud jazz music, and people dressed in colorful outfits, Dalton and Juan decided that their favorite shop was on Royal Street—John H. Cohen & Sons. It had been in business since 1898 and had gold and silver coins, ancient armor, and all kinds of firearms and swords, including medieval long swords, European rapiers, and Arabian scimitars. But the ones that fascinated them the most were the sabers, the swords with large, curled hand guards and gently curved blades, the ones used by pirates like Blackbeard and Jean Lafitte, whom they had already heard so much about on their visit. What stories the boys could make up standing among all this antique weaponry.

The store was not busy that day, so the teenage boys were able to talk to the curators and learn all about the cutlasses and black-powder muskets and rifles. Both Dalton and Juan had visions of pirates in their thoughts and dreams after learning about the past in history class and reading books on pirates for reports they had to write. In the glass cases in the middle of the store were old coins dating back to biblical times and in a case by itself sat a gold "pieces of eight" or Spanish doubloons, pirate's treasure. Dr. Miller had to drag the boys out of the store as it was closing, thanking the sales people for their patience.

Afterward the three of them headed down Saint Louis Street toward the riverbank to see the Mississippi. Standing on the levee, they watched as boats of every size sailed up and down its muddy waters. Even a white riverboat with its big paddle wheel passed tooting its horn. Then Juan saw a person wearing a Hard Rock New Orleans T-shirt with a pirate on it.

"I'm starving and that shirt is 'lit,' " said Juan. "Can we go there to eat? I want to buy a shirt to add to my T-shirt collection."

So, Dr. Miller and the boys headed north to the Hard Rock Café where they gorged themselves on huge juicy burgers and fries and a drink the waiters called Pirates Poison. After cheesecake, they walked back to their hotel exhausted and full, but still making up stories about pirates and pretending to sword-fight. As soon as their heads hit the pillows, they were out.

Off early the next morning, the boys saw Mobile, Alabama, as it went by and then Pensacola, Florida, with its white beaches and great condos, but nothing compared to their day in New Orleans. Even as they turned south on Interstate 75, they kept thinking about Cohen's. They saw signs for Disney World, Kennedy Space Center, and even what was once the winter headquarters of the Ringling Brothers Circus, but the conversation quickly returned to New Orleans. Even as Interstate 75 turned east in what is called Alligator Alley, the boys could not stop dreaming of pirates long enough to see its infamous residents. The pirate bug had bitten them, and they could think of nothing else.

Everglade City was their final destination and their new home for two months. Their excitement increased when they saw Jungle Erv's Airboat Tours on their left, with its big red-lettered sign and its flat-bottomed boats.

"Look at the size of that motor and fan," screamed Juan. "I have never seen anything like it. How does it work?"

"They mount a car-size engine in a long, flat boat and attach the huge fan to blow the boat along the water," Dr. Miller explained. "The fan works better than a propeller because it will not get stuck in very shallow places."

"We have got to try that!" the boys exclaimed in unison.

A few blocks farther down the street was the Everglade City Motel, a tan-and-white single-story complex. The office was in the center of the property with a large fountain in the front and a sitting porch to the right. Dr. Miller parked the car and they all went in. It was not fancy like some big hotel in Dallas, but it had a homey feel to it with comfortable chairs and a long desk to register. Mr. Sam Langston, the owner, reached over the counter and shook hands with all three of them.

"Welcome to the Everglades. Is this your first time to visit the glades?" he asked.

The boys said yes, but Dr. Miller told the owner that he had visited there years ago when he was still a grad student.

"Y'all are from Dallas?" asked Mr. Langston. "Well, Everglade City is going to seem mighty small, but we have a lot of things you boys will enjoy this summer. I will try and point y'all in the right direction."

"Thank you," the boys replied.

"Dr. Miller, you reserved a room with two queen beds and a kitchenette," Mr. Langston said. "It is number five just around the corner. You can park the car right in front and your boat along the side of the building. Feel leave the trailer there if you like. I will be around to keep an eye on it for you."

"Thank you, Mr. Langston, for everything. I'm sure we will get to know you better as the summer goes by and we will return the favor," Dr. Miller appreciatively replied.

Dr. Miller parked the car and then opened the door to Room 5. It was clean and as described had a small kitchen with a refrigerator and a microwave, two queen beds, a dresser with a TV, and a bathroom.

Nothing fancy, but the room included everything they needed to eat, sleep, and play.

After Dr. Miller, Dalton, and Juan unpacked, they went down the street to a café for dinner. Afterward, the boys were still excited about the days to come. But exhaustion from the drive won out, and they were soon tucked in bed dreaming of ships, sails, and alligators.

Chapter 4

Exploration

No one got up early the next morning. Dr. Miller and the boys were tired from the drive, and the silence of the swamp surrounding the town was so tranquil compared to the city. Dr. Miller awoke first and drove down to a convenience store to pick up some basics for breakfast. He planned to drive to Carnestown later that day to do some real grocery shopping. The boys awakened with excitement and then ate powdered doughnuts and drank milk jabbering about what they wanted to do today. They decided to stay together and explore so Dr. Miller would begin his research the following day.

It looked as if a fog had taken over the room as Dalton's dad made them put on mosquito repellent as he said, "If the gators don't get you, the mosquitoes will."

They laughed spraying one another and then choking on the smell.

"The gators might be a better choice than the bug spray," quipped Dalton, laughing.

Mr. Langston, the motel owner, was out watering the plants in front of the office when they came out, so they walked over.

"Where should we begin with our exploration of the area, Mr. Langston?" Juan asked.

"Well, I can smell the bug spray, so that is always the best place to begin," he laughed. "The oldest place with any history would be out on Chokoloskee Island. The Indians use to stay out on that island and even the military used it back in the 1800s for a camp. There is no telling what y'all will find out there."

Then the motel owner suggested the boys might take an airboat ride out into the swamp so they could see the surrounding area. He reminded them that they would be in swamp territory, so they had to be careful. They should not be surprised to not only see alligators but to find them in the middle of the street or right where they wanted to go.

"Remember to be patient and wait or go the other way because even though they appear large and slow they swim faster than any human and run almost as fast," said Mr. Langston.

The boys thanked the motel owner for his advice and promised to be careful. Then Dr. Miller, Dalton, and Juan got into their car to drive out to the park and marina.

"Alligators in the street, are you kidding me?" Dalton exclaimed. "That's like *Crocodile Hunter* stuff. Do you think he was just kidding with us, Juan, since we're from Dallas?"

"Man, I don't think so," replied Juan. "We came in on a road they call Alligator Alley, and we saw gators along the way. Now we are on the edge of the swamp. I think he was being truthful."

"So, what do we really do if we are approached by a gator?" asked Dalton.

"I don't know about you, but I'm out of there!" Juan exclaimed.

Up to this point, Dr. Miller was just listening to this conversation without saying a word. Then he decided to egg it on a little.

"Which one of you is the fastest?" he asked the boys.

Juan laughed and said, "I am."

"Then, Dalton, you have a few choices," said Dr. Miller. "Always be looking around for them, try to run faster, or throw Juan to the gator so you can get away."

When Dr. Miller ended his advice with a smirk, everyone started laughing.

Still feeling nervous, Dalton took out his phone and Googled "what to do if you run into an alligator." Here's what he found: 1) Be aware around water; 2) Keep your distance; 3) Never feed or entice an alligator; 4. If it starts to attack, run in a straight line away from it, since they run about as fast as a human, they tire easily so you can stay ahead of them; and 5) If attacked, fight back.

Everything except the running in a straight line made sense because Dr. Miller had always heard to run in a zigzag pattern to get away. These items were duly noted and discussed. Dalton's father had been around swamps for years since he was always studying in some kind of marshy area and carried a gun when he went out just in case, but this was all new to Dalton and Juan.

Dalton had never been on a swamp trip with his dad before.

Dr. Miller continued the drive to the island. He and the boys didn't see any alligators despite looking intently for them. The road went west from Everglade City with the swamp on both sides of them as if they were driving on a finger of land in the middle of water. They then came to a long bridge that sent them arching over the water to the island. The island was not large, but there were still plenty of people in RVs and even tents along with houses for rent lined along the water.

They turned right into the marina and there met the owner, a Native American by the name of Nokosa-bear. His complexion was dark from working in the sun all his life, and he had a bright toothy grin that seemed to be permanent on his face. Though he appeared to be in his seventies, he still looked as if he could whip a bear in a fight. Everyone knew him. He was one of those people who attracted visitors and conversation. He would regale anyone willing to listen with stories of the Indian tribes who lived in the area and their history not as someone who read about it but instead as someone who had lived it. He was still working because he loved people and couldn't imagine doing anything else.

After introducing themselves to Nokosa-bear, Dr. Miller and the boys began to ask questions about the island's history, a subject Nokosa-bear loved to talk about. As they sat on the dock, he told them stories of the Indians who had lived in and around the area, how they often gathered on the island because of its beauty, and how the U.S. Cavalry had tried to catch some of them but they were able to hide on different islands. He talked of the great fishing off Chokoloskee, kayaking in the mangroves, and even about Dead Man's Rock. The boys asked about alligators on the island, and he was glad to explain that because salt water surrounds the island the alligators didn't come out this far. The boys were ecstatic, and they all rented kayaks from Nokosabear to tour the area.

It was hard for the boys to get the hang of kayaking since you had to paddle on both sides. They found that you went around in circles if you only paddled on one side. Juan didn't have as much trouble figuring out how to balance and paddle his kayak, but Dalton was a different story. Since he was taller, his center of balance was higher, and he almost immediately turned over his kayak much to the laughter of his father and Juan. Then he had trouble getting back into his kayak; it rolled over every time he tried.

"Hang on, son," his father said as he paddled over to hold his son's boat steady while Dalton to crawled over the side.

Juan laughed and joked, "At least there were no alligators watching. They may have thought you were squirming bait!"

Before too long, the three of them were racing along the coastline. The water was crystal clear, as if they were looking through a glassy window. They could see everything below them, from fish to rocks and even the occasional orange starfish. It was a lot different from being in the muddy lakes around Texas where you couldn't see your feet even if you were standing in three inches of water. With their new adventure and open seas, they splashed and played their way in and out of small bays and through the mangroves. When they turned west around the south end of the island, they felt for the first time the rise and fall of the blue waves and the gusty wind of the Gulf of Mexico seemingly driving them backward. They had not realized how much rougher it would be on the windward side of Chokoloskee Island. Until they changed direction, they had been paddling almost effortlessly, but now they were using more strength and effort as the waves splashed over the bow of the kayaks shooting a mist of water into the air and directly into their faces.

Feeling a little tired, Dr. Miller coaxed the boys to the shore for a short rest. After beaching their kayaks, they began to run along the shore kicking sand and chasing each other.

To have all of that energy again, thought Dr. Miller as he watched Dalton and Juan run along the soft white beach laughing and teasing each other.

Running backward and messing with Dalton, Juan tripped over a large rock and Juan tumbled down with a huge thud.

"In all of this white sand, you have to fall over the only rock in sight," Dalton bellowed as he reached down to help Juan up.

Juan scooped a handful of sand and threw it at his friend for the comment and then they walked back to Dr. Miller.

Heading toward their kayaks, the boys laughed and told Dr. Miller about what had happened. He gave them a strange look.

"This beach is all sand and you stumbled over a large rock? Could that be Dead Man's Rock?" Dr. Miller asked the boys. "You know the rock that Nokosa-bear was talking about in his story?"

It had not occurred to Dalton and Juan. But when they checked the area and saw no other rocks, they both stood and shrugged their shoulders with an "I don't know look."

"Well, it almost killed Juan, that's for sure," snickered Dalton.

They waded back into the shallow water and slipped into their kayaks heading back toward the marina and to Nokosa-bear, staying on the leeward side where it was smoother. Completely exhausted by the sun and their newfound love of the water, they returned the kayaks, got back in the Jeep Grand Cherokee, and drove to a café in Everglade City for a late lunch and then back to the motel to rest.

The minute they got back to the hotel, Dr. Miller collapsed on the bed and went straight to sleep while the boys broke out their electronic devices to see what the rest of the world or more specifically what their friends were posting on their Instagram accounts. Nothing real exciting just the ordinary activities of middle school kids, but they did learn that some friends were following their adventures in Florida through the boys' posts. More than one friend had asked about the pictures of alligators the boys had posted and wanted to know if they were going to kill one for some Texas-size alligator boots.

With his phone still in hand, Juan decided to check out Nokosa-bear's stories and some more of the history of the area. He twisted his head and felt a sharp pain reminding him of the somersault had done over that lone rock. He searched the Internet for the story of Dead Man's Rock and only to find a short excerpt from a Seminole history account that talked about the Indians finding a man lying crushed on the rock hundreds of years before.

Could that have been the same rock that I tripped over? he wondered. He would have to ask Nokosa-bear the next time they were together.

After his nap, Dr. Miller drove them all into Carnestown, a larger town deeper into the mainland, to go grocery shopping. What teenage boy would find grocery shopping exciting, Dalton and Juan were thinking until they realized that they got to pick out food they wanted to eat. Licking their lips with huge grins on their faces, they eyed the Takis corn chips and sodas and filled the basket almost full of junk. Dr. Miller didn't complain; instead, he made sure there was plenty of healthy food in there as well.

When Dr. Miller and the boys got back to the hotel, Dalton and Juan unloaded the Jeep while Dr. Miller began cooking spaghetti. After gorging themselves on two helpings, the teenage boys settled down to watch the beginnings of the NBA finals. No one they liked was in it, but they watched anyway cheering and screaming at the referees as if their voices could be heard through the television. Exhausted, they each crawled in bed to dream again of the adventures they would have.

Chapter 5

Eaten with Fear

When the teenagers awoke, they realized it was their first day on their own. Dr. Miller had gotten up early, packed a quick lunch, and drove to the ramp across the street to launch the boat. It was his first day to begin his research, so he headed into the swamp with snails on the brain. Since his goal for the day was just getting an idea of the area, he let Dalton and Juan sleep and gave them the day to explore. He left a note on the refrigerator with instructions:

Good morning. I am off to look around the swamp and cultivate some areas to search. Please take your cell phones with you and let Mr. Langston know where you are going. Be careful and have a great day. See you this afternoon.

With instructions read and understood, they poured themselves bowls of sugary sweet cereal and headed out to visit Mr. Langston.

He was out in the parking lot sweeping up some trash when they approached him.

"Good morning, guys. What do y'all have planned for today?" Mr. Langston called.

"We haven't decided yet," Dalton replied. "What would you do?"

Thinking for a bit, Mr. Langston said, "I have a canoe behind the motel that you boys can use if you wear life jackets, stay away from gators, and let me know which direction y'all are headed. Carry it across the street and up the road and launch it there in the bayou. I figure I would paddle it east. Then when it starts to narrow a little, turn right. I wouldn't go too far on your first time out, but y'all can at least see what it looks like around here."

After the boys exchanged cell phone numbers with Mr. Langston, they thanked him and ran behind the motel. Excited to begin their adventure, they found the canoe, paddles, and life jackets right where he said they would be. The boys pulled the upside-down canoe down from the sawhorses, took the life jackets and paddles off the pegs nailed to the wall, and then lugged all of it across the street. They headed for the spot Mr. Langston had described, set the canoe down on the edge of the water, and donned the life jackets. Dalton had played around in a canoe at church camp the previous year, so he put Juan in the front and then slid the canoe out into the water, jumping in at the last minute.

It looked like a cartoon with them rocking the boat and paddling in different directions. It seems so different from the kayaks the previous day where the teenage boys had to paddle on both sides and were sitting almost on top of the water. As they shifted around in the canoe, they leaned too hard on one side, so water started coming in. Their first reaction was to jump back, but that just caused it to do the same on the other side.

With their feet soaking wet, Dalton yelled, "Sit down, Juan, or we're going to be gator bait."

Both boys settled into their seats with their hands holding each side of the canoe to steady its rocking. After a minute, the boat calmed down, so they tried to paddle again, taking only a few minutes to figure out they had to work together. When they were ready, they paddled out past the swamp tour stand and then turned right as the bayou narrowed.

The water was brown and murky, but at least it was smooth and easy to paddle in. They were in awe of what they saw along this quiet strip of water that seem to be disturbed only when the oars sent out rings of waves. Occasionally, a fish would break water with a splashing sound, and it caused their hearts to beat at twice their speed. The water seemed to flow straight out of the grass and cattails along the bank. There were plants and lilies growing in the shallower water, creating flat plate like leaves that rolled up and down with each wave that passed by. The white flowers stood erect like periscopes with a white bloom that opened and pointed at the sun. The constant buzz of the katydids was always around filling the air with while the call of the birds seemed to echo on forever. There were some low trees and tall brush, but much of what they saw was tall green grass or patches of lower grass where the cattails had forgotten to grow.

The farther they went into the bayou, the more they began to see all kinds of wildlife: herons, big rat-looking animals called nutria, and even a small alligator.

They stayed away from it even if it was small. Even with all of its sounds and dangers, the bayou had a peaceful feel that seemed to stop time and envelope them in a calm that the city never allowed.

As Dalton and Juan paddled farther away from Everglade City, they gradually began to hear the sounds of the swamp. They had never experienced anything that quiet before, so different compared to the noise of Dallas. The silence was almost deafening as they stopped paddling and just floated for a while. A splash broke the silence as they saw an alligator enter the water from the right-hand bank, peering after a small bird that was lazily floating on top of the water. They watched in awe as the alligator leaped out of the water with its mouth wide open and clamped down on that unsuspecting bird with the fury of a storm and the cunning of a tiger. Where there had been a bird enjoying the lazy day, now all that was left was the water boiling from the alligators thrashing as it dove back under the water. They had only seen the viciousness of an alligator on YouTube so they both sat there in stunned silence. It seemed like it took an hour before they were able to move. With eyes as large as doughnuts and mouths like gaping fish, they turned to each other with expressions of pure shock. The one thing they knew was that they did not want to stay around much longer, so they dug their paddles into the water and rowed in unison as quick as they could to get away.

They paddled back toward Everglade City and the motel. When they finally got the nerve to talk, it was only for directions. Neither Dalton nor Juan could express what they had just seen. Life was snatched away in the blink of an eye, and nothing was there to stop it. It was obvious both boys were playing that scene over and over in their minds, and each time it was as if the alligator had jumped up and grabbed their tongues out of their mouths and their hearts out of their chests.

Mr. Langston told them they could just leave the canoe, life jackets, and paddles on the shore if they planned to go out later that day. Without a word spoken between them, the boys simultaneously picked up the canoe, carried it back to the motel, and set it back on the sawhorses. Neither one of them wanted to eat lunch, so they played Halo for a while but did not talk about what they had seen.

As soon as Dr. Miller walked in, he knew that something was wrong. He expected them to be jabbering nonstop about their day. Instead, they were silent, even as they played their video game, speaking only when they had to speak.

Not beating around the bush, Dr. Miller questioned, "What has made you two magpies so silent?"

It seemed like a flood of emotions rushed into the room like a tidal wave crashing hard against the beach. At the same time, the teenage boys started talking about what they had seen. They spoke as if the words were burning in their mouths and they had to get them out; otherwise, their tongues would be permanently seared.

"Stop, I can't understand anything you are saying!" demanded Dr. Miller.

Juan immediately stopped and Dalton began to tell the story.

"We went out in Mr. Langston's canoe this morning," said Dalton. "It was amazing after we figured out how to keep from tipping over the boat. We paddled out past Jungle Erv's and right off of the bayou, just like Mr. Langston had directed us to do. We were completely amazed at the wildlife and the swamp and the way the water meandered through the grassy islands. It was like nothing we had ever seen before."

Then Dalton described the tall grass, the brown water, and the quiet compared to the city. He told his dad that he and Juan were soaking it all in when an alligator stealthily slipped into the water and swam up to an unsuspecting bird floating out away from shore. In a horrifyingly swift move, the alligator snapped up the bird before their very eyes. They were shocked, surprised, but most of all frightened by the pure power and speed of the alligator on the unsuspecting prey. Their only instinct, after they snapped back to reality, was to get out of there as soon as possible.

"We haven't really talked since that moment, Dad," Dalton said. "We just paddled home and sat here in a daze."

Juan blurted out, "What if that had been one of us?"

The questioned lingered as they sat there still in shock hours later.

Dr. Miller sighed as if understanding what they had felt and the fear that was still in them. He did not want to think about what would have happened had it been either of them; that thought became too painful for him also. It was not his first time in the swamps since snails flourished in places like this, and in fact he had had plenty of encounters with alligators and other predators over the years.

"We learn from our mistakes and watching the mistakes of others," he told the boys. "In this case, it was better that it was the bird instead of you, but now you have seen firsthand how dangerous the swamp can be."

"Do you have any tricks that have helped you, Dad?" asked Dalton.

"Here are some that have kept me safe," said Dr. Miller. "I poke around in the water and in the grass with a stick before I get in, so that there is not one lying on the bottom just waiting. I also wait before I get in, making sure that I know where the alligators are and how to safely get away from them. I rarely step into water much over my ankles, but since they move so fast, even that is not safe. And you can't see them coming in the brown water, so I keep that big stick handy to beat them off if I must."

"Can we use our paddles?" asked Juan.

"Don't use your paddles," cautioned Dr. Miller. "You will need them to get away to safety. I also carry my pistol with me for protection. It is illegal to hunt alligators, but you can shoot them for your protection."

Then Dr. Miller told the boys about the story from his college days. One of his professors took the class on a trip to the swamp and had an alligator hunter show the students how to work around them and be safe in the swamp. A guy named Mike got too close to the water, and an alligator lunged out at his leg. He screamed and the rest of the students turned around to see the alligator trying to drag their classmate into the water. Mike used his walking stick to start clubbing the alligator in the head. A guide nearby grabbed another stick and hit the alligator in the eye. This caused the animal to release Mike's leg for a moment, which was long enough for Mike to drag himself away. The guide continued to hit the alligator's head so it slipped back into the water, and they were able to get Mike to the hospital in time to stop an infection. It was scary to see a friend being bitten by an alligator, but it was the quick thinking of the guide that saved Mike's life. So, from then on, they did not walk without a stick in their hands or without a friend if they could help it.

"Since I do so much of my research by myself," Dr. Miller said, "I always keep a sharp walking stick, my pistol, and a large knife to stab any alligator behind the eyes if I have to."

The boys sat listening intently in utter amazement at what Dr. Miller was telling them. Knowing that the best way to survive anything was to consider all possibilities and make contingency plans, the teenagers discussed with Dalton's dad what they should do and what they needed to survive an attack if it happened. They talked about how to avoid the alligators on the shore, and what to do if one swam at them; what each would do if the other person was attacked and even who to call on their cell phones.

Dr. Miller decided to take the boys to the Walmart in Carnestown in the morning to buy them hunting knives just to be safe. It all made for a long and frightening evening so the boys went to bed early. Sleep was not easy to come with visions of that bird continuing to replay in their heads.

The next morning after breakfast, they went into Carnestown to pick up some groceries and shop for knives. Standing at the counter in the sporting goods section at Walmart, they gawked at all of the different guns and knives, and it brought back memories of the shop in New Orleans. After looking at every type of knife available and talking to the sales clerk who had lived in the area all of his life, the boys each chose a Whetstone Tactical Survival knife with a sheaf. The knife had a six-inch razor-sharp blade with jagged teeth. The handle contained a survival kit and a working compass, which might come in handy in a difficult situation. Strapping them on their belts, both Dalton and Juan felt like buccaneers ready to face anything.

After heading back to the motel to drop off groceries, Dr. Miller suggested they spend the rest of the day with him out in the swamp. Though hunting snails was not their idea of fun, they were honestly too scared, even with their knives, to venture out on their own. They climbed into Dr. Miller's boat and headed out. The boys' heads were spinning like tops trying to keep their eyes open for more alligators while clutching the sheaths of their knives on their hips. Dr. Miller sat in the back of the boat, laughing to himself while he watched Dalton and Juan shake, squirm, and fidget as they kept an eye out for the prehistoric-looking beasts.

"When we get to where I'm researching, I'm going to need you to put on waders and get out of the boat as we hunt for snails," said Dr. Miller. "Since there are three of us, we can walk the nets along the shore while everyone pulls the net and looks for alligators. We are not going in deep water because the snails stay in the reeds and shallows, so the first thing we are going to do is make sure the edge of the water is clear."

"How are we going to do that without getting eaten?" cried the boys in unison.

"Well, the plan is to draw straws and have the loser jump out of the boat and run up and down the bank real fast," Dr. Miller chuckled.

With wide eyes and a shocked look on their faces, they sat speechless. Dr. Miller reached for straws and then told them to draw, but they refused.

"Okay, if no one wants to run on the shore, how about we throw these rocks I have in the bucket and see if we can scare them off instead," Dr. Miller told them.

The boys eagerly grabbed rocks and started peppering the shoreline with them. You would have thought that it was a hailstorm as they continually blasted the water and grass with rocks. After a few minutes and a couple of scares from birds flying off, they put the boat ashore at an open spot where they could see at least thirty feet into the surrounding area. Dr. Miller climbed out first with his stick and then jabbed around in the water along the shore. Nothing! The boys heaved a sigh of relief and then got out of the boat, carrying the sticks they had found near the boat launch. They stabbed their sticks into the water and then stood in the shallow water, spreading the seine net between them.

"I feel like I'm standing over my fish tank at home with that little blue net we use to scoop up dead fish and junk," declared Juan.

The teenagers were surprised at all the things that wound up in the net—small fish, seaweed, and several snails—but glad that an alligator was not part of their catch. They quickly got back into the boat for safety as Dr. Miller scooped up the snails and the boys threw the fish back into the water. Dalton's dad placed the snails in a container, pulled out his GPS, wrote down the coordinates of where the snails were found, and made some other notes in his book. He seemed pleased with the samples, and after seining a few more times, he and the boys headed back to the motel.

"Wow, I never thought hunting snails would have been this scary!" exclaimed Juan. "I thought it would have just been see some snails on the weeds, grab them, and you were done. I had no idea how dangerous it could be or even the number of notes that were taken about each snail as we found it."

"This was a first for me because any other time we have been collecting specimens it was in small ponds or clear water lakes," replied Dalton. "We did watch for snakes, but that was not like having to keep an eye out so we were not eaten."

The teenage boys had learned a lot, not just about Dr. Miller's work but about survival and how to take some extra precautions if they came across any alligators. Each boy felt a little braver when it came to going back into the swamp, but both now had a new appreciation for how dangerous their forays into the swamp would be.

Chapter 6

The Find

For a few days, the boys hung close to the motel. Playing video games, watching movies, and kicking the ball around the parking lot consumed most of their time. Neither one would admit it, but they were still apprehensive about going back to the swamp. They were better equipped than before with their knives and with their survival tips, but they were still hesitant to put them to the test.

"I'm bored, so why don't we go kayaking near the island," suggested Dalton. "There won't be any alligators because of the salt water."

Juan agreed, so the boys got on their bicycles and headed to Chokoloskee Island to visit with Nokosa-bear.

"I'm glad to see you boys again. What adventures have you been on?" inquired the old Indian.

The boys felt comfortable around this wise, old weather-beaten man. There was just something that made you trust him with your thoughts. The boys began telling him all the excitement they had had and even their fears about alligators and the swamp.

"I remember when I was young I went through those same feelings: fear, excitement, and even embarrassment. We were living off the land, but we knew the land could just as easily live off us," Nokosa-bear exclaimed. "Often I was not sure if I was hunting them or they were hunting me in the swamp. A number of times, I thought I was about to become a meal. But I kept my cool and stuck to what I had learned, and it paid off for everything except my thumb."

He then held up his left hand with his thumb curled out of view. With an awful gasp, the boys' eyes grew as round as moons and almost as white. Laughing, Nokosa-bear popped out his thumb, wiggling it to their astonishment and then their laughter.

"Boys, the swamp can be dangerous," Nokosa-bear reminded them. "But from what you have told me, you have learned a lot about survival. You know how important it is to be cautious and expect something to happen. That way, you are either ready or disappointed when it does not happen."

The boys nodded their heads in agreement.

"Where are you boys headed in the kayaks?" asked Nokosa-bear. "Don't waste this pretty day. Get out and explore."

"We thought about paddling out to that sandbar just off the island to do a little snorkeling," said Juan.

"It's a great place to snorkel and splash around," Nokosa-bear offered. "The tide is on its way out, so it should be exposed, and any sharks will be farther out catching the fish moving with the current. It should be pretty safe. Put your phones in the watertight box and call me if you run into any trouble. My number is in the box."

The boys thanked him and then they picked up the kayaks, moved them to the water, and then slid in with a push from their new friend.

"Did he have to bring up sharks?" whined Dalton. "Just about the time I'm getting a little more comfortable with alligators, we add a new animal that wants us for dinner."

"Well, we are part of the food chain, though I just always thought we were at the top," laughed Juan. "On land, we appear to be at the top, but around the water we drop down to a main course so that makes you a white meat chicken and me an enchilada."

"At least that gives me a chance," snorted Dalton. "You know everyone loves Mexican food!"

With that, the water fight began. Slapping their paddles at an angle produced a good-sized splash, so the boys proceeded to drench each other as they laughed and hollered.

Before too long, they were back to using the paddles to move the kayaks instead of using them as instruments of war. With the outgoing current, Dalton and Juan were able to move swiftly away from Chokoloskee and out to the sandbar. The tide was almost out, so the water did not push them out past the shallow strip of land that usually was three or four feet underwater. After about twenty-five minutes, they were sliding their kayaks up onto the sandy finger of land that had been underwater hours before. There were all kinds of sea life fighting to get back to the water when they arrived, so they sat on their boats for a while watching the crabs and one lone starfish slip back into the depths. They never realized how much the tide rose and what its effect was on the creatures that lived in it. It was amazing as each thing adapted to the twice-a-day moves of the tide, still continuing to flourish. The teenagers decided to see what else moved around after the tide, so they put on the masks they had brought and waded out into the water.

The salty water was warm and clear that June morning with the sun shining through the water and waves creating a greenish blue tint. It had never occurred to Dalton or Juan what made the ocean water the color it appeared to be. The boys suddenly realized it was the sun and the reflection off of the bottom that gave it the different hues. It was so clear they could see fifty feet away until everything turned to a blue haze. They floated over the sand like clouds hovering over the ground looking down at all the things below. A couple of stingrays scooted across the sandy bottom moving away from the boys' shadows like kids running from dark rain clouds for fear of getting wet. It all seemed so unreal as they gazed into a world they had not experienced before. If the fish world believed in aliens, then one was tall and white with bright orange shorts, and the other was shorter and tan with the red and gold of his favorite soccer team. That would make their kayaks their mother-ship so maybe they were aliens watching and catching specimens to eat.

The more they breathed through the snorkel, the more it seemed as natural as standing on dry land. With the buoyancy of the salt water, they floated with little effort as if skydiving but never reaching the ground.

The floating was only interrupted when one of the boys dove to the bottom to take a closer look at something that attracted his attention. A deep breath and then a head pointing toward the bottom with their hands pulling the water past their bodies and their feet kicking for as long as they could hold their breath gave them entry into this other world. A few times, it was a bright fish or a small school of fish swimming along; at others, it was the sparkle of something in the sand that caught their eyes and off they went underwater to scope it out. Most of the time, the thing they went after was something that a fisherman had left behind: a rod, a basket, and several beer cans. It made them wonder how fishermen ever got back to shore with their fish if they were so drunk they left the fishing gear in the sea. The boys continued their exploration around the south end of the sandbar enjoying the feeling of freedom and the excitement of a new escapade and no thoughts of that long-tailed prehistoric-looking beast that had frightened them a few days before.

After an hour, the boys swam back up to the sandbar to sit and relax for a while. They sat on the edges of their kayaks as the waves created a rhythmic sound. It was as if nothing else in the world mattered as these best friends experienced a calm they had not felt before, a calm produced by being totally alone and totally free of any cares. They had thought to take some bottles of water with them, so they drank and sat discussing all of the things they had seen so far.

Their excitement was hard to contain as they talked about all of the fish and coral, far more than they could describe. Their imagination began to run away when they started conjuring up the things that they could find on the bottom of the gulf. The list ran from dead bodies with concrete tied to their feet to sunken ships with treasure, each inspired by movies they had seen.

Before too long, they were headed back out into the water to finish the loop around the sandbar they had started earlier that morning. The teenage boys were busy talking and not watching where they placed their feet when Juan kicked something. First he thought it was a rock. It was just his luck to find the only rocks on the whole island again, but out where they had been walking there was only sand. Mad that his foot hurt, he reached down to grab the rock and throw it as far as his muscles would allow him. But instead of a rock, the object felt very different. Juan got down on his knees, put on his mask, and dipped his head in the water to see what had made him stumble. It seemed to be a piece of wood about two feet long, which was covered in moss and sand. He fanned away the sand and waited for it to settle. The board seemed odd, not like any board he and his father used for building things in their backyard. It had tiny holes as if some creatures had bored through it. Juan lifted the board out of the water just as Dalton walked over to see what his friend was doing.

"What did you find, Juan, a piece of Noah's Ark?" chuckled Dalton.

"I'm not sure, but it's worth taking back to the motel later to show your dad," Juan replied. "Maybe we can make something of it as a souvenir from our summer."

Juan set the board inside his kayak and then the boys continued snorkeling for an hour longer, chasing fish and playing giant alien to the rest of the sea creatures. The sun was now well over their heads, and their stomachs were telling them it was time for lunch. They headed back to the marina on their kayaks. When they arrived, Nokosa-bear was gone, so they carried the kayaks back to their cradles and headed toward their bikes.

"How are you going to carry that board on your bike?" asked Dalton.

Juan stopped; he had not thought about riding home with it.

"I don't want to throw it away," said Juan. "Maybe we can find some rope to tie it on my bike."

As Juan walked back to the Dumpster at Nokosa-bear's, his hand brushed off some of the moss. To his surprise, he saw some kind of design, a brand of some kind. It seemed faintly familiar to him, but he could not figure out was it was or where he had seen it.

"Dalton, you have got to see this. There is actually some brand or something on this board," Juan proclaimed.

Dalton walked over and looked down on it with furrowed eyes as if squinting to see what was on the board. Something looked familiar to him.

"Juan, you know that poster in your room with all of the old soccer logos on it," said Dalton. "Doesn't this look like one of them?"

"Are you saying this piece of driftwood is from a soccer club?" laughed Juan.

"No," said Dalton. "But something about the shield and the crown look like some team logos. Look at it real close."

"You are right. I look at those posters every day in my room and didn't even notice it," remarked Juan. "This one does look a lot like the logos from the Spanish league. Let's take it back to the motel and see if it is one."

Luckily, the boys found a few pieces of twine in the Dumpster and decided they could use it to tie the piece of wood to Juan's bike. After it had been secured, they peddled back to the mainland and to their motel.

As soon as they arrived at the motel, they ran inside to grab some Hot Pocket sandwiches to squelch that screaming hunger they had been experiencing since they left the sandbar. They then gulped down two sodas, went back outside, untied the board from the bike, and carried it over to where Mr. Langston had left the garden hose. With a brush they found behind the motel office, they began to wash and scrub away all of the crud on the board until it was clean. Dalton pulled out his phone and took a picture of it and posted it on Snapchat as their great find of the trip. The boys put it on the patio to dry while they grabbed their phones to search the Internet. Starting with old logos Juan remembered from the soccer poster hanging on his wall, they found out they were similar to the coats of arms used by Spanish kings. Juan told Dalton that the Spanish word *real* means "royal." So they researched crests dating back through the centuries. And as they went back in time, they seemed to be getting closer to the one on the board. When they found the one used by King Ferdinand II and Queen Isabella I, it was almost a perfect match. That meant that the wood had come from the early 1500s. They could not wait to show the board and their research to Dr. Miller when he came in. Their minds immediately started to imagine all of the things it could have been.

Late in the afternoon, Dr. Miller came back to the motel tired and smelling of snail guts. He had been out on the edge of the swamp collecting samples and was completely exhausted. His hope was for a quiet evening with his son and Juan watching TV or playing video games as he collapsed on the couch with his feet propped up on the coffee table, the thing his wife, Linda, would not let him do at home. But the teenagers had other ideas. They had been dreaming all afternoon of what the board could be, inventing stories wild enough to make their English teachers proud. Before Dr. Miller could even sit down, he had an old smelly piece of wood shoved into his face and became engulfed in the excited chatter of the two boys.

"Okay, slow down, I can't understand both of you at the same time," demanded Dr. Miller with his hands up in the air while shaking his head back and forth.

Juan spoke first since he was the one who found the board.

"We were out on the sandbar north of Choko-loskee today when I stumbled on this piece of wood," Juan said to Dr. Miller. "First I thought it was a rock, and then I realized it was an old wooden plank. When I dug it out of the sand and we cleaned it up, Dalton thought the insignia looked like the logo on from a soccer club poster on my wall at home. We got on the Internet and found that it matches the insignia of King Ferdinand and Queen Isabella of Spain from around

1500. We have no idea what it is from, but it seemed like a weird place to find something so old."

Juan exhaled as if he had just run a marathon when he had finished.

Dr. Miller thought the boys had been joking, so he had not taken them seriously. But his eyes widened and his jaw dropped when he saw the connection between the piece of wood and the royal crest. It took him a few minutes to gather his words. Dr. Miller had discovered some amazing things as a scientist but none of them were as surprising as what his son and Juan had found.

Dr. Miller got out his phone and called Southern Methodist University, hoping to catch someone in the archaeology department. But his friend Dr. Fernstein was on a dig in South America at an Incan sight with no phone service.

Thinking that the plank could be a significant discovery, he told the boys, "You have found something, but it is hard to tell what. It may be better if we did not share this yet but keep it under wraps until we can find out more."

The boys agreed but then remembered that Dalton had posted a photo on Snapchat.

"Well, I don't think that will be a problem since it went to your friends and not out into the public. We should be pretty safe," assured Dr. Miller. "Let's put together a plan to discover what this is, where it is from, why it was out on the sandbar, and if there is any more out there."

The boys agreed and then listened to Dr. Miller's ideas on how to proceed.

"I think we need to get more information on King Ferdinand and Queen Isabella and their ties to this area," said Dr. Miller. "We will most likely have to go to the library at the University of Miami to complete our research."

Then he wondered out loud about carbon dating. Would they be able to check the wood's authenticity? Brainstorm what it came from? Dalton also wanted to search the sandbar to see if there were any more pieces and include Nokosa-bear in the project since he had more knowledge about this area than anyone else.

The boys realized that their summer just took a crazy and exciting turn, but Dr. Miller reminded them that he still had to continue his research on the snails in the area. So, the three of them decided to take turns working on both projects.

"I will help you with yours," Dr. Miller told Dalton and Juan. "And the three of us will go out to work on my research, which should help me complete it in one third of the time and give us two thirds of the time to find out about your plank."

That sounded fine to the teenagers. They would have agreed to anything.

That night, the boys split up the things that needed to be researched. Dalton checked out King Ferdinand and Queen Isabella, and Juan looked for their connections to Florida. Both made great headway as Dr. Miller cataloged his snail findings. Finally, around midnight, the boys faded off to sleep and Dr. Miller turned off the lights. He did not know if this was a true find or just something for the boys to play with, but he knew now that the boys would have something to keep them busy and would definitely make the rest of the summer eventful.

Chapter 7

The Adventure Begins

The boys understood that Southern Methodist University was paying Dr. Miller's expenses and therefore their expenses in Florida, even though they wanted to go back out to the sandbar, they went to the swamp to hunt snails. But nothing stopped them from dreaming and talking about what they had researched the night before. That helped them get through the day quicker and made standing knee-deep in muck with a net almost bearable.

The boys learned a lot about snails as they pulled the little slimy creatures out of the nets and placed them in containers. They learned that snails are hermaphrodites, which means that they have both male and female organs. Snails look for mates when they are a year old, and then they both lay eggs. Dr. Miller was studying this mate-selection process. He wanted to determine what criteria snails used to find a mate. The boys laughed and said it was who had the fanciest shell or who was the fastest if they were sticking with the survival of the fittest theory. They determined that speed could not be a factor since snails measured speed in days not seconds.

They made a lot of snail jokes while they worked, and Dr. Miller egged them on. He even told some of his corny snail jokes:

Why doesn't McDonald's serve escargot?
Because it is not fast food.

Or what happens when two snails get into a fight?
They slug it out.

Dalton and Juan just snorted and splashed water at him because the jokes were so dumb.

On the way back to the motel, the teenagers planned their evening research. Dalton had discovered just about all he could concerning King Ferdinand II and Queen Isabella I, including the fact that at this time Spain was sending explorers out and financing their trips. Now he wanted to research Spanish explorers in the 1500s around Florida and the Caribbean, but the only name that seemed to make sense was Christopher Columbus. Juan Ponce de León came to Florida much later.

Wow, he thought, *I'm researching real history that we have studied in school.*

Looking up from his laptop, he shared the information with Juan. That night, the boys' research was more focused than before. They found that the Spanish king and queen had commissioned Columbus so everywhere he went he claimed the territory for Spain along with any valuables he found. Realizing they were doing history "homework" during their summer break made both of them laugh. For the first time, history had become real and even personal. What would Mr. Bagwell say?

The next day, they were able to focus on their project. After breakfast, the boys and Dr. Miller loaded up their boat and went out to Chokoloskee Island. They decided to search the area around the sandbar first. And if they found anything, they would share the results with Nokosa-bear. The tide was on its way out, so they hustled to put the boat in the water and get out to the sandbar. With the boys' guidance, Dr. Miller beached his boat closer to where Juan had stumbled on the piece of wood. The three of them looked but didn't find anything, so it seemed that there was nothing else to find.

Frustrated, Juan said to Dalton, "Hey, I just walked in that area."

"Are you sure?" asked Dalton.

Juan nodded. "I'm positive. Have we all been searching in the same place?"

Then Dr. Miller suggested that they separate so they could search a larger area and not waste their time looking in the same place over and over again. They used some water bottles they had brought and some cans to mark off areas, and each one searched just inside of his assigned space. They realized they were covering a lot more ground this way. They found a lot of other things—conch shells, jellyfish, more fishing equipment—but no more wood.

After about three hours, the boys were hot so they decided to snorkel instead of walking around in the shallows. While snorkeling, they spotted something brown about seven feet below them. Dalton went down to check it out, and to Juan's surprise he brought up not just one but several pieces of wood. They swam with the pieces between them until they could stand up in the shallows. Then they carried the wood to a dry spot on the sandbar and began to scream for Dalton's dad to come and see what they found.

Dr. Miller was searching another area they had marked off. He hurried over with a big smile on his face.

"You guys find some more wood?" Dr. Miller asked the boys.

When Dalton and Juan held up the pieces, Dr. Miller realized what it was.

"It's a barrel. Look, with these pieces, you can see the place where the metal rings were and even see that they are still curved."

The boys could not believe it; they were holding a barrel from the 1500s. The piece they had back at the motel looked like it would fit perfectly. They put the barrel pieces in their boat and continued their search. They stopped when the tide began to come back in and hurried back to the boat to head to the marina.

Twenty minutes later, they were loading the boat on the small trailer when Nokosa-bear came out to greet them.

"Have a good morning?" inquired Nokosa-bear.

"In fact, we did have a good morning and would love to get some information from you about our find," replied Dr. Miller.

Nokosa-bear walked over to the trailer in the parking lot and leaned his elbows on the boat's rail.

"You know if I can help you I will. What kind of information do you need?" he asked Dr. Miller and the boys.

A little apprehensive to share their findings, Dr. Miller took the lead.

"The boys found a piece of wood the other day out on the sandbar," he told the old Seminole. "They were about to throw it back when the noticed its logo. A stamp on the wood looked familiar so they borrowed some twine out of your Dumpster, tied it to their bikes, and brought it back to the motel. After a little research, they found that the wood was old so we went back out today and found three more pieces that looked like they would fit together."

"How could you tell they were old?" asked No-kosa-bear.

"The piece of wood had a brand that was used during certain years. I know you know the history of this area. Do you know of any reason why there might be a five-hundred-year-old barrel in this area?" Dr. Miller sheepishly asked.

"How old? Did you say five hundred years?" Nokosa-bear shouted. "Now that would be a find. I know that Juan Ponce de León once explored this area. Could that answer your question?"

"We thought the same thing," replied Dr. Miller. "But the crest was not used after 1502, and Ponce de León did not land in Florida until 1513. Could it have been anyone else?"

"Our thought was Columbus, but we are not sure he came here. None of our research shows that," said Juan.

"Wow, you guys have done your research," No-kosa-bear said, complimenting the boys. "Not to my knowledge, either. Ponce de León gets credit for exploring Florida. I guess your barrel could have fallen off of a ship and floated to here. It seems like a long way but not completely impossible."

The teenagers pulled out the wood that they had found and cleaned it up in the marina for Nokosa-bear to see. Now it was even more apparent that the pieces fit together along with the four discolored lines that indicated where the metal rings had been once. Crusted on the end and still holding them together was what was left of one of the rings. It was rusted and pitted but partially still intact. The rivets were still holding fast to one of the boards. The four of them examined the wood with awe. To think that someone had hand-cut each piece of wood and fired each metal band that held the barrel together more than five hundred years ago.... Could the craftsman have imagined that two teenage boys would have found what he created so many centuries later?

For the four of them it was an intense feeling, like they were standing in history. But the mystery still remained: How did it get here?

Dr. Miller, the boys, and Nokosa-bear sat in the marina eating lunch. They talked about the history of the area, parts of which the Seminole had shared with them the first time they visited Chokoloskee. Even though it wasn't about the 1500s, they still enjoyed the conversation.

Just as Dalton was putting a Coke bottle to his lips, he stopped with a strange look on his face.

"Didn't you tell us about the man found out by that rock on the end of the island?" he asked the native Floridian. "When did that happen?"

"I had forgotten about that. The Seminoles do not measure time the same way as the white men, but it was well before the arrival of the armies and others whom the Indians fought and hid from," Nokosa-bear said. "You might have stumbled onto something. Why don't we take my truck and ride out to that spot?"

They all loaded into the truck, locking the barrel pieces in Nokosa-bear's office for safekeeping. The island wasn't very large and Nokosa-bear had a cool four-wheel drive, so they made it to the spot where the legend said the Indians had found the man. Then they walked over to the rock and brushed the sand away from it.

"How are you sure this is Dead Man's Rock?" asked Juan. "There have to be other rocks out here, what makes you so sure this is it?"

"Look at the rock," said Nokosa-bear. "See how it has a large rounded shape and then seems to just fall off. The Indians said that they found the man against a rock that looked like his funny-looking large nose. Can you see the resemblance?"

It looked more worn than it probably had when the Indians had found the man, but they could still see the silhouette of a nose.

"Indian noses don't look like that," said Nokosa-bear. "For them, it seemed funny and easy to remember."

That made sense to the boys and Dr. Miller, so they sat there thinking. *What would the barrel and this man have in common? How could the man be here and the barrel be out there? Where did the man come from?* Now they had more mysteries to solve, but they all agreed that there had to be some connection between them.

"Do you think we should look around here to see if the rest of the barrel is close by?" asked Dalton.

"Now that the tide has come back in, we are limited to what we can see on land, and that's not much," Nokosa-bear confessed. "When we get back to my marina, we will look at the tides and see if there is a good time to search."

All four agreed and climbed back into the truck. As soon as they were at the marina, Nokosa-bear gave them Cokes from his refrigerator and then they checked the tide chart. The tides moved daily, but they determined that the best time during the day for the search was in four days, so they made plans and then said their good byes. Nokosa bear agreed not to say anything to anyone about their find. After spending time with the old Seminole, Dr. Miller and the boys knew his promise was good, so off they went back to the mainland to the motel and after dinner and video games off to sleep.

Chapter 8

Research Trip

With four days to wait, they decided that the most productive use of their time was to get up early and head to the University of Miami Library. The boys normally would not have been too thrilled to spend their summer break at a library, but instead they were pumped. The little bit of research they could do on their phones and computers had opened their eyes up to what might really be an exciting mystery. Trying to solve the mystery became their great quest.

During the three-hour trip to Miami, they talked about what they had found and what questions were still unanswered.

"Boys, I know you have watched mystery shows or police shows on TV," Dr. Miller said. "We need to begin to think like and even act like the detective who is trying to solve the case. Every idea we have we need to chase down until we found the answer."

He warned the boys that they would find not only answers but new questions that would need to be answered. And they would have even more clues to chase down. He urged Dalton and Juan to write down all of the sources they used, including what they had found to date.

After hearing his father's plan, Dalton complained. "You don't want us to make a bibliography, do you? We did that while writing research papers in English. It seemed so useless."

"Believe it or not," said Dr. Miller, "you will use this bibliography because it will help you remember things you have read. You may need to go back to that same place. I'm betting that we are going to look at a lot of different books and articles, so if you don't write it down, how will you know where to go?"

He cautioned the boys about a situation where they would come across a stream of thought and remember reading something about that in a book but not find which book it was they had read. Then they would have to do twice the work just because they did not make a note of where they had read that idea. He compared it to him going out in the swamp on the main bayou but all along the way there are smaller streams. Each idea is like a stream, and he would go up it until he couldn't go any more, then turn around, go back to the bayou and look at another stream until he found the one that answered all his questions.

"If you do not write down each stream, someone may go down that stream again and waste time, or there may have been something down a stream you went down that needs to be found again," said Dr. Miller. "So that is why we write it down or create a bibliography."

The boys agreed it would be dumb to not list the books and the information in case they had to go back.

"I guess I never knew how important that bibliography could be. I just thought it was busy work," sighed Juan.

About an hour outside of Miami, Dalton's phone rang. It was Chase, a friend from next door. They had gotten to know each other by playing catch in the yards and riding bikes to school.

"Hey, Dalton, how's your summer going?" asked Chase. "I saw your Snapchat. It looked like you guys were having a great time."

"Yah, we are. We are headed to Miami this morning," replied Dalton.

"Really? I've always wanted to go there. Did your dad's brother get a hold of him?" asked Chase. "He seemed like he was anxious to see him."

"My dad doesn't have a brother, Chase," Dalton answered. "You must have been mistaken."

"Well, your mom wasn't home, and he saw me playing in the yard," said Chase. "So, he introduced himself as Dr. Miller's younger brother and said he was trying to find out where he was researching this summer. I told him you guys were in the swamps in Florida, but I didn't know where. Are you sure he doesn't have a brother?"

"Dad, you don't have a brother I don't know about, do you?" asked Dalton.

"No, I'm an only child. Why would you ask me that?" he replied.

"Chase said a man came by the house saying he was your brother and asking where you were," replied Dalton.

"That's strange. What did this guy look like?" asked Dr. Miller.

Dalton thumbed the speaker button on his phone and asked Chase to describe him.

"He had dark hair and a mustache and was about the same height as your dad," said Chase.

"Chase, this is Dr. Miller," said Dalton's dad. "What did you tell him?"

"That you guys were in the swamps of Florida looking for snails, that was all I knew," answered Chase.

"Chase, I don't have a brother. Please call us if this guy shows up again," said Dr. Miller, very perplexed.

"I will. Have a great time in Miami," answered Chase, and then he clicked off the phone.

"That was strange. Why would anyone be looking for me? They could have called the university to see where I was researching. But I guess this time of year it's hard to get anyone to answer since only a few classes are being taught. Why would they say they were my brother?" Dr. Miller wondered out loud.

"Could it have been one of your friends trying to play a joke on you but not realizing you were gone?" asked Juan.

"No, I just have a few colleagues I work with, and outside of that not a lot of friends, especially ones who don't know where I am," replied Dr. Miller.

His mind began to whirl, trying to think of anyone he knew that fit Chase's description of this mysterious "brother." Dr. Lieberman, whom he shared an office with, was short and old and nice, but he, too, was out doing research this summer in Idaho.

Another great mystery, thought Dr. Miller.

Dalton and Juan were mystified as well.

Dr. Miller and the boys put it out of their minds because they were getting into Miami traffic. The conversation turned back to the pieces of wood, the research, and eating Cuban food for dinner.

They had traveled across Florida on US 41. As they got closer, the GPS sent them south on State Road 826, then east on State Road 878. They began to see signs for the University of Florida as soon as they turned on US 1, which ran up the Atlantic coast. Dr. Miller parked the car near the Richter Library, the general library on campus and checked in using his SMU credentials. The card gave them access to all areas of the library, not just where the public or the University of Miami students could go.

Dr. Miller found the history section, and the boys commandeered a table. There were very few students in the library during the summer session, so they were able to talk freely since hardly anyone was around. They looked up Florida history from the 1500s on the catalog computers. Ponce de León came up. In fact, US 1 was also called Ponce de León Boulevard. They checked their dates to make certain that he was not in Florida at the time. They did chase the thought that he had barrels that were ten years or more older on his ship, but that seemed unlikely. When he would have set out, he would have had fresh supplies. And since he landed on the Atlantic side, it did not make since he would have carried old barrels across the state. A dead end "stream" but one they noted, along with where they had found the information, in their "bibliography."

Dr. Miller had begun researching the old Indian claims and stories. After a while, he found the story that Nokosa-bear had told them about the dead man on the rocks out on Chokoloskee. Looking over the time line of chiefs that a researcher had created and the mention of the story, it appeared that the dead man must have been found around the early 1500s. That seemed to fit with the date of the barrel pieces, which Juan had set out to research again to make certain the dates were accurate. This time, they made copies of the pictures that matched the logo and even of barrels discovered from that time period. They all seemed to match the size and looks of the pieces they had found.

So far, their research had agreed with what they had already uncovered, but now they were making copies of the places they were finding things and keeping up with the bibliography, so they did not reduplicate their work. They made stacks for each of their findings: Indians, Explorers, and Barrels. The stacks grew as they found more material and made copies or printouts they felt were important. Periodically, Dr. Miller would look over what the boys ascertained and help them decide whether to keep looking or move on to another "stream." Surprisingly, the boys became good at doing the research. In fact, Dr. Miller thought that the boys were doing as well at researching as his graduate assistants at SMU, the students who were working on master's and doctorate degrees who graded, researched, and even taught some of the lower-level classes. Both boys felt good about the compliment. No longer did they think how boring it was to be in a library during the summer. They were actually having fun.

After a few hours, they took a break and ran to McDonald's. It was not Dr. Miller's choice, but it had been weeks since the boys had eaten fast food. It was close by the campus, so after some burgers, fries, and McFlurries they headed back to the library.

They had been researching for another hour when Dalton said, "There just doesn't seem to be anything that points to Spanish explorers being in Florida that early."

Dr. Miller agreed. But where did they go from there?

Juan was just closing a book when he noticed a map in the back cover that showed Florida and the Caribbean.

"Do you think someone accidently came to this area of Florida?" he asked.

They had talked about that a little bit before but never put it into the context of coming from the Caribbean.

"That might be a possibility, but they would have been sailing the wrong way to get to Spain," Dr. Miller noted.

"Who was in the Caribbean from Spain at this time? Maybe it fell off of a ship and ended up here," questioned Dalton.

With that thought, they went down another "stream" of thought to find out about the explorers in the Caribbean. Most of them came to Florida after 1517: Álvar Nuñez Cabeza de Vaca in 1527, Alonzo Álvarez de Pineda in 1519, and Pánfilo de Narváez in

1527, but none as early as 1502. The mystery still stood but they were at least eliminating possibilities.

Dr. Miller focused on Columbus and saw that some of his men had landed on the mainland of Mexico and had raided several Mayan cities there, but had always retreated back to the islands Columbus had discovered first. They must have created their own civilization on the islands and that made them feel more at home. He also found a place where the author had mentioned some of the storms that hit the Caribbean.

Dr. Miller said, "What if it was not on purpose, but a storm blew the ship off course and the barrel came off of the ship?"

Juan asked, "How could we be certain of a storm that would push a captain that far off course and in the 1500s?"

"We would have to know the weather patterns and even the flow of the ocean to determine that," Dr. Miller answered.

Holding up a brochure he had picked up when they came into the library, Dalton said, "The university's marine and atmospheric library is not too far away. Wouldn't they have records of storms?"

Sure enough, the Rosenstiel Marine and Atmospheric Library on Virginia Key was only a few minutes away. Everyone agreed a change of scenery would do them some good, so they collected all of their research and off they went.

Along the way, they picked up some drinks. When they arrived at their destination, they found a whole school out on the key with classrooms, library, weather station, beaches, and docks with research boats. The large white building did not look like a boring library.

"I think I would like school more if it was on a beach," laughed Juan.

After walking up the front steps and through the glass doors of the library, Dr. Miller gave his credentials to the librarian. Then they were taken to an area where a graduate student manned the atmospheric desk.

"Do you have weather patterns and records of storms for the 1500s?" asked Dr. Miller.

"Yes, but only from records created by ships and people who went through them," replied the young man behind the counter.

What a strange question for a malacologist, thought the grad student. But he laughed it off and helped them look up that information. There were several major weather events in the Caribbean around the early 1500s according to their records. The largest of the storms was in July 1502. That storm did major damage to many of the islands and it was noted that there were numerous ships lost.

The boys both looked at each other but did not say a word. The grad student was busy talking to Dr. Miller and did not see the boys' reaction to hearing about confirmed storms. From his quick description, it seemed like a big storm around July 1502 were perfect fits for the barrel, and to top it off the report of numerous ships lost added more possibilities to their search.

Could one of those ships have been pushed away from the Caribbean and into the Gulf of Mexico? Where did it end up?

Was it intact as it got close to Chokoloskee? both Dalton and Juan wondered.

Then Dalton asked, "Do you know the path of the storm in 1502?"

The grad student pulled up some atmospheric maps from the time period with markings for areas that they had confirmed there was damage. The recorded path showed damage in Santo Domingo also known as Hispaniola and on into the current island of Cuba. The boys traced the path asking about whether it would have been considered a hurricane and what path they generally would take. The grad student was happy to oblige them by pulling up a graph of hurricanes over the last one hundred years and isolated those that seemed to head in the same direction. The path most often went straight into the Gulf of Mexico, which would mean that a boat trapped in it could have easily ended up on Florida's western coast. They nudged Dr. Miller without saying anything and caught his attention. He had not made the connection that the boys had made until they quietly pointed it out to him. They thanked the grad student for his help and then retired to a quiet corner of the library.

"It all seems to make sense, the storm, the ships lost, and the date seem to all be pointing at the same event that could have brought our barrel and our mysterious dead European to Chokoloskee Island," Juan said the moment they were alone. "They don't seem like coincidences and I think are worth looking into."

They agree and began looking at ships that were recorded lost in that storm in the marine portion of the library. They were astounded to find that twenty-eight out of thirty-two ships were lost from a fleet of ships leaving Santo Domingo on July 1, 1502. With that many ships, the odds were the barrel and the man were from that fleet. As they continued to search, they came across the harbormaster's ledger with a manifest of those ships, and it appeared they were all carrying items of value to Spain. The list included tobacco and other products. But more importantly, it included gold.

"Did this trip just turn into a treasure hunt?" Dalton asked with disbelief in his voice.

"I think it may have," responded Dr. Miller.

The spent another hour exhausting any other leads they found and then packed up their papers and left. They checked into a hotel not far from the university for the evening, found the Little Havana section of Miami, and gorged themselves on *ropa vieja*, plantains, rice and black beans, and flan. Sleep didn't come easy, but it did finally come with dreams of treasure.

Early the next morning, they checked out of their hotel with all of the research they had done. Then with great expectations, they headed back to Everglade City and Chokoloskee to see what they might find. The trip was uneventful except for having to stop once to let an alligator finish crossing the highway, something you would never see in Texas.

Chapter 9

Sifting in the Sand

The first day back, they had to focus on Dr. Miller's research, since the last two had been spent on the pieces of wood. Dr. Miller didn't mind taking time off from his work, especially where the boys were concerned, though he did have to answer for the grant money he was using for his research. The boys knew that Nokosa-bear thought they should meet in four days to have the longest and lowest tide to search, so a day chasing snails seemed okay with them.

Today, Dr. Miller, Dalton, and Juan went by boat into an area where extra eyes and hands would help Dr. Miller. They went about two miles deeper into the swamp, farther than the boys had canoed the first time. The reeds were high, and the constant hum of the bugs, croaks of the frogs, calls of the birds, and that always scary splash of an alligator chasing something seemed to be the norm. They ran the boat aground in a place where there weren't any reeds and the ground was flat enough to see a gator if it were close by. This time, they carried buckets and clippers instead of nets. They were walking along the shoreline looking for the snails in the vegetation.

As before, the boys cautiously got out of the boat with their sticks and knives, keeping an eye out for alligators. Dr. Miller had told them that alligator nests are usually away from the water and if they had eggs or babies, Dalton and Juan needed to be even more careful. You would have thought that the boys' heads were able to spin completely around the way that they were turning and watching. Lucky for them, they only heard some gators in the distance but none close by.

Dalton and Juan spent the day collecting and talking about what they would do next on their research. It seemed that every time they found a snail and noted its location, it would remind them of the barrel pieces and other possible outcomes—buried treasure, pirates, galleons, etc. Most of all, they dreamed of finding the answer to the riddle of the barrel pieces and what other artifacts they could find.

After about five hours in the swamp, Dr. Miller and the boys started to head back. It is unusual to run into people in the swamp because it is so large and not many people visit one unless they are on a tour or hunting alligators illegally. Today, they passed a boat that carried two men with binoculars. They guessed if you could look for snails, you could also look for birds and wildlife, so they did not give it another thought. But down deep, Dalton had a strange feeling: that feeling you get when you know something isn't right but can't explain why, when the hairs on the back of your neck begin to rise and shivers go down your spine. He didn't say anything to his dad or Juan because he wasn't sure if it were the men or the alligators that were disturbing him. He just quietly stored that thought away.

When Dr. Miller and the boys returned to the motel, there was another car in the parking lot. Even though it was summer vacation season, not many people were staying at their motel, so they took notice. When they saw Mr. Langston out watering again, they visited with him as they always did.

"Looks like you have more guests tonight," Juan said to Mr. Langston.

"Two fellows came in wanting to go out into the swamp. They rented a room just after you guys left this morning and went down and rented a boat to go out," said Mr. Langston.

"That must have been who we passed a little while ago," Dalton said.

"Did they say what they were doing?" asked Dr. Miller.

"They told me that they wanted to get out of the city and see the swamp, is all they said," replied Mr. Langston. "I almost gave them the same warnings I gave y'all, but they didn't act like they wanted any advice so I let them be."

It took quite some time to document what Dr. Miller and the teenagers had found in the swamp and take pictures of each specimen. Very few of the snails would go back to Dallas with them; most would be returned to the swamp, so detailed data and documentation were critical for Dr. Miller's research. After they were finished, they cleaned up and went to get something to eat. After handling snails all day, no one was interested in cooking. Later in the evening, it was back to the motel, a little video game time and then off to sleep, which did not come easily with all of the exciting ideas running through their heads.

Dr. Miller, Dalton, and Juan were set to meet Nokosa-bear at seven the next morning, because of the tides, so the boys were up early, anxious to begin their search. Nokosa-bear believed that this would be the easiest time to find anything since the water was shifting the sand. They ate breakfast, packed a lunch, drove off with the boat, and were on Chokoloskee at the marina a little before the designated time. Nokosa-bear was there waiting for them. He asked one of his friends to manage the marina while he was gone, so he could be with them all day, if need be, to search.

"It's going to be a great day, no clouds, steady seas, and a gentle breeze," he said to Dr. Miller and the boys.

Then pointing to Dr. Miller, he continued, "I think we should split up in order to increase our search area. Each of us takes one of the boys in a boat. I will search Dead Man's Rock and you go back out to the sandbar."

"That does sound like the most efficient way to cover the territory. Juan, are you okay going with Nokosa-bear?" Dr. Miller asked.

With a big smile on his face, Juan nodded yes. He had been fascinated by the old Seminole and was excited to spend more time talking to him.

"Let's take one of my boats so we can get away from the shoreline more easily," Nokosa-bear suggested to Juan.

The two headed to the dock while the Millers off-loaded their boat from the trailer. Each wished the other luck and made an agreement to leave their phones on so as to call the other if they found anything. If they needed help or found more articles, they would call and not get on the radio to keep their find quiet. They motored away together and stayed side by side until they reached the end of Chokoloskee, then the Millers went west toward the sandbar, and Juan and Nokosa-bear went east to toward the island.

Nokosa-bear anchored the boat just offshore, so they would have a platform to rest and hopefully some place to store what they found.

"I think starting out here makes the most sense," commented Nokosa-bear. "People have walked this beach for years, so the chance of finding something is small. But out here, the water is always moving things around."

"That does makes sense," Juan said while slipping off his T-shirt and grabbing his mask. "I'll begin to search this area on the left side of the boat if you go on the right."

He spit into his mask to keep it from fogging up and slid over the side of the water as Nokosa-bear did the same thing on the other side. Even though Nokosa-bear was in his seventies, once in the water he was as agile as Juan, maybe even more agile.

The two began to search, swimming in straight lines then turning and swimming back to not miss anything. The water was not more than twelve feet deep, so they could easily snorkel along the top and dive down to check out anything that looked interesting. With the water this clear, it was as if they were swimming along the bottom. After searching their respective areas, they came back to the boat and decided they would now search the areas in front of and behind the boat. An hour and a half later, they both climbed up into the boat tired. Nokosa-bear pitched Juan a bottle of water to drink and took a long swig of the bottle he had just opened.

"Did you see anything interesting?" Juan asked while twisting the cap off of his water bottle.

After a long swallow, Nokosa-bear replied, laughing, "Nothing to do with the boat but the fishermen sure lose stuff."

"Dalton and I said the same thing last time we were out looking. Is that the reason why you sell fishing gear at the marina?" said Juan, poking fun at the Seminole.

"I told you I was a wise old Indian," snickered Nokosa-bear.

Juan was enjoying the time together with the Indian. He reminded him in some ways of his grandfather. Not just the age but the laughter and the stories made him immediately feel at ease. Juan checked his phone and saw no messages from Dalton so he and Nokosa-bear had a snack and sat while being rocked by the gentle waves. Juan told the Seminole about what they had found in Miami: about the huge hurricane that struck the Caribbean on July 1, 1502, and about the number of boats lost. From their research and their own conclusions, both Dalton and Juan felt that all of this fit in their time line. Juan also said that they were able to confirm the story Nokosa-bear told about Dead Man's Rock being at about the same time period by a man who researched through tribal records. The most exciting thing was that the boats that were lost were carrying valuables for Spain.

Juan said excitedly, "What started as a mystery may turn out to be a treasure hunt."

"Well, at my age, the mystery is more interesting than treasure, but a little gold might brighten my day," Nokosa-bear chuckled.

In the meantime, Dalton and Dr. Miller had anchored just south of the sandbar and had chosen areas to search. This was the first time this summer that both father and son had been alone together. It was great having Juan along, but Dalton did miss the alone-times with just his dad. After they searched for a while, they too, sat in the boat and talked. Dalton had helped his father collect samples before, but now that he was older he was beginning to understand more of his father's work. Dalton told his dad how glad he was that they had moved to Dallas. He liked his school, he liked his soccer team, and he had met his best friend, Juan. Things could not have been better. Dr. Miller was relieved to hear that. Moving a teenage boy is never easy, but he had felt all along that accepting the position at SMU was the right decision for the whole family.

All of a sudden, Dalton got that strange feeling again. He looked around but didn't see anyone or anything. Yet he just felt that someone was watching. After a few minutes, he turned to his dad.

"You know when Chase called me about the guy claiming to be your brother," he told Dr. Miller, "I got a weird feeling. Then when we saw the guys in the swamp, I got the same feeling. It was as if something strange was going on."

Dr. Miller listened intently as his son continued.

"I know this sounds strange, but I think they are connected, Dad," said Dalton. "That both instances of people showing up unexpectedly are related. Here's the stranger part, I'm getting the same feeling right now but I don't see anyone around."

Dr. Miller thought about it for a minute. He did not see how or even why the two instances would be related. No one would be spying on them; they had only found some pieces of wood and not told anyone except Nokosa-bear. But he did not want to discount his son's feelings.

"Why do you think they are related other than the weird feelings?" he asked Dalton.

"I don't know," Dalton said worriedly. "No one knows what we have found so no one would be after us for it. Nokosa-bear would not have told a soul. It just doesn't seem to fit with his nature, so I agree they could not be related. I still have that feeling that I cannot shake."

They both sat for a while thinking about the feeling and the events that had happened. Occasionally, they would look around but didn't see anyone.

Then Dr. Miller and Dalton both went back into the water to search again in other areas. The activity kept Dalton's mind off of the weird feeling, and the swimming gave him the sense of freedom he enjoyed. Periodically, the scientist's son would dive down but not find anything interesting. The other pieces of wood he and Juan had just stumbled across easily, but searching purposely seemed to be a pain. Like most teenagers, Dalton liked getting things. But he didn't enjoy putting a lot of effort into anything except soccer. Several times, he wanted to stop searching and just play, but he knew that everyone else was still searching and anyhow he wanted to find out the origins of the barrel. So, like a team player, he swam on searching.

Out of their view, the two men from yesterday were watching with high-powered binoculars. There were no boats left to rent except the one that Nokosa-bear was in, and they would have been spotted immediately out in the water, so they chose to stay on Chokoloskee Island where they had been able to follow and watch from a distance. Their employer had instructed them to stay close but do not engage. They were being paid to find out whether the wood they had seen on Snapchat was real and if they had found anything else of value.

James Farmer and Nick Barnes worked private security for a Mr. Charles Lanning out of Boston. They usually were doing background searches and surveillance of clients and competitors of Lanning's many businesses. It did require them to travel and to sit, as they were doing now, for long periods of time just watching and making notes. Farmer, now in his early fifties, had been a marine and then gone into police work when he got out of the service. A friend of his had told him that private security work paid a lot better than being a police officer, so he changed careers. Barnes was much younger. He had played football in a Division 2 college, which accounted for his size, but he had also gotten a degree in computer engineering. He was a whiz at anything that was technical and that is what made Farmer and Barnes a good team. Today, that team happened to be hiding on a beach watching a father and son snorkeling. Barnes's computer programs had caught the Snapchat picture, and now their boss had sent them to see if there was more.

After picking up a rental car in Tampa, Farmer and Barnes drove down the coast toward Everglade City to begin their surveillance. In the car on the way, they received a message saying that Dr. Miller and the boys had gone to the University of Miami's Library for Marine and Atmospheric Sciences to do research. The grad student had been on Mr. Lanning's payroll for a while. His job was to let Farmer and Barnes know if anyone inquired about things that would lead them to one of the sunken caravels, apparently a hobby or dream of Mr. Lanning. Farmer and Barnes had made the mistake of being seen in the swamp, and they could not afford to make that mistake again. It was a real problem because there was only one motel in the area, the one where the Dr. Miller and the boys were staying. So today it was crucial that they not be seen by any of them. Thankfully, the mangroves along the shore kept them well hidden.

Between the snorkeling and the sun, everyone was getting tired on both boats. Dr. Miller and Nokosa-bear had spoken to each other once during the day to see what kind of progress either had made, but all had come up empty. The tide was already beginning to come in so each boat agreed to make one more grid search before they called it a day and went home. Nokosa-bear and Juan had moved the boat farther east to look, hoping that more of the ship had floated just past the island. Juan was swimming back toward the boat when he saw something brown on the bottom. He had been disappointed several times already today, so this sighting did not get his hopes up, but he dove down anyway. As he got closer, he saw that it was wood covered in moss. He had to come up and take a second breath because the water was deeper due to the incoming tide. This time, he went down straight and brushed the sand away. Immediately, he saw that it was more of the barrel. It seemed to be buried deeper than he thought, so he popped up excited. When he surfaced, he saw that Nokosa-bear was already in the boat drying off.

"Nokosa-bear, I found something, but I can't get it by myself," said Juan.

Nokosa-bear pulled up the anchor, started the motor, and moved closer. It didn't make any sense to him to leave the boat to swim over and then have to drag whatever they found back to the boat. Juan was glad Nokosa-bear was moving the boat because he was getting tired. He clutched on to the side of the boat when it pulled up to rest while Nokosa-bear dropped the anchor.

"What do you think you found?" asked Nokosa-bear.

"I think I found the rest of the barrel. It's covered in moss and it's buried deep in the sand. We may need something to help unstick it," panted Juan as he treaded water.

Nokosa-bear reached under his seat and pulled out a small shovel like campers use.

"I keep this around just in case my anchor gets stuck," said Nokosa-bear. "It's a great pry bar."

The Seminole handed the shovel to Juan and then slipped over the side of the boat to follow the teenage boy to the brown object. They both took a deep breath and submerged to the bottom. There lying in the sand were more pieces of barrel. Juan immediately started to dig out around them with the shovel while Nokosa-bear fanned the sand away from another area so they could see what they were doing. Professional treasure hunters use a vacuum type of hose that deposits the silt away from the area, but these two amateurs used what they had. After three attempts to get the sand cleared away, they found more than the rest of the barrel. Something that looked like a box was lying protected under the curved edges of the wood. Juan took the barrel pieces to the boat while Nokosa-bear gently picked up the box. But as soon as it was in his hands, he knew that it was something different. Surfacing, he swam quickly to the boat where Juan was already sliding the rest of the barrel over the side before getting into the boat. As Nokosa-bear arrived, Juan leaned over to take the other object out of the Seminole's hands and place it in the boat. As the "box" came out of the water, Juan saw that it was something wrapped in cloth. Setting it down on the seat near him, he waited for Nokosa-bear to get back in before looking any closer. He did not want to disturb the wrapping or what was inside the package. He did go and check out the pieces of wood he had loaded, and it was indeed the same type of wood with the same markings but more intact than the first pieces they had found.

"Do we open it?" Juan asked.

"Well, it won't open itself," Nokosa-bear said sarcastically.

"What kind of cloth is it and how come it's not ruined?" asked Juan.

Unfolding the cloth, Nokosa-bear explained, "There were no watertight containers back in the old days. If they wanted to keep something from getting wet, they wrapped it in oilcloth, which was usually cotton or linen woven very tight and then soaked in boiled linseed oil. If wrapped enough times and tied tightly, the oilcloth was almost impervious to water."

Then the Seminole borrowed Juan's knife and cut the strip binding it together. As he removed layer after layer of the cloth, he became more convinced that he was holding a book, possibly a ship's log. Finally, removing the last layer, he held in his hand a very damp but not soaked book. For fear of losing any of the contents, he gently rewrapped it and placed it in an emptied fishing tackle box while Juan called Dalton. The four of them agreed not to open the book until they were altogether and in a place where it would not be easily destroyed.

Each boat pulled up its anchor and headed back to the marina. The Millers arrived first and were putting their boat back on its trailer. Nokosa-bear and Juan got there a few minutes later and pulled up to the dock. Dalton could hardly contain himself, but they had decided not make a commotion given the circumstances. Juan passed the tackle box up to Dalton while Nokosa-bear tied and covered up the barrel pieces. They all went inside the marina, locking the door behind them. Whatever they found, they believed they should do it in private. Luckily, the men watching the Millers did not see Nokosa-bear and Juan. And not believing anything was found, they left Chokoloskee Island before the Millers returned to the marina.

Chapter 10

The Log

Though anxious to see what was in the book, Dr. Miller, the boys, and Nokosa-bear waited until they were all together in the store. This way, no one else might hear or see what they had found. Slipping quietly through the door, they passed by the lures, fishing poles, and counter, before entering Nokosa-bear's private office, where they gathered around a long folding table. After they cleared off the stack of papers and marine parts, Dalton carefully set the tackle box on the table. No one spoke or even reached out to touch or open the gray-and-orange box. You would have thought that it held a poisonous snake. It was not that they were scared of the box; they were in awe of the fact that they had found something they thought was more than five hundred years old, so they didn't know where to start. They wondered if the book would be so soaked to render the pages unreadable. Everyone wanted to know, but no one wanted to be the one to let the other down with bad news.

Finally, Dr. Miller stepped forward, put his hand on the box, and looked at his son, Juan, and Nokosa-bear for approval. It only made sense that the one scientist, even if he was a malacologist, should open and handle the book. Nokosa-bear's hands were old and rough from the wear of hard work, and the boys were too young and careless to open such a delicate thing. No one had to say it. Dr. Miller was the right choice, so each nodded for the scientist to take the lead and open their prize. As the boys held their breath, Dr. Miller unlatched the handle and swung away the metal hasp to fold the lid of the box back, exposing the contents.

Before Dr. Miller could touch the book, Nokosa-bear quickly handed him some latex gloves, which he kept in his medical box. Perhaps an old crime movie had given him the idea. Dr. Miller slid them on and proceeded to remove the book. To all of their surprise, the old leather and parchment paper had not turned into mush. The book was still rigid. Dr. Miller slowly unwrapped the oilcloth from the book, gently rolling the book to expose each and every layer of cloth—four in total, to give maximum protection. After Dalton's dad removed the final layer, they all saw the book's simple leather binding, and its size not more than eight, inches long five inches wide, and an inch thick. The embossed letters on the cover were not completely legible; only a couple were visible because of age and use. Nokosa-bear dabbed some moisture away from the cover using some rags he had in his office. Cautiously and gingerly, Dr. Miller opened the book to reveal about around a hundred pages of yellowed paper that were damp but not soaked. Whatever was on the pages may still be legible.

Everyone leaned in close to get a closer look. The ink had run some but the ornate letters were distinct enough to read. However, the words were in Spanish, not English.

"Juan, how fluent are you in Spanish?" Dr. Miller asked.

"I have spoken Spanish all my life, but I have trouble reading it," Juan replied.

"I took Spanish when I was younger and learned to read enough to pronounce words," said Dr. Miller. "But I don't have a large enough vocabulary to tell you what they mean. So here's my thought, if I read the words the best I can out loud, Juan, see if you can translate or at least get us close to a translation."

It seemed like a good idea to everyone so the slow and often unintelligible translation began of the first page.

"*Este es el diario de navegación de* El Dorado. *Una caravela de Su Majestad el Rey Fernando II y Su Majestad la Reina Isabel I de España. Encargada en 1500 en las Atarazanas Reales de Barcelona,*" pronounced Dr. Miller in a very slow voice.

"This is the navigation diary of *El Dorado*. A caravel of His Majesty King Ferdinand II and Her Majesty Queen Isabella I of Spain. Some word I don't know in 1500 at the Barcelona Royal some other word I don't know," translated Juan.

"Hey, this might be easier than you thought," Dalton quipped to his best friend.

"I think *diario* means 'log' instead of diary, Juan," corrected Dr. Miller. "The first word that you didn't know, *encargarda*, may mean 'commissioned' since that is what you do when you launch a ship in the service of a country. Let me check Google translate for *ataranzanas*."

After he found out that *ataranzanas* means "shipyard," Dr. Miller continued reading aloud for Juan to translate. But no sooner had they translated the first part, did they have to stop. Juan didn't understand the next section, and they couldn't find a translation on their phones that made any sense to them. It appeared that some things were going to be a mystery until they had the log professionally translated. The last thing on the page that could be read was the captain's name, Antonio de Torres.

They had discovered a lot in just one simple page: the name of the ship, when and where it was built, and the captain's name, which gave them someplace to begin to focus their attention. Even if the rest of the pages were illegible, they at least had a chance of finding out why the barrel, the log, and possibly one of the crew ended up in Florida. Everyone was talkative and excited about what they had found.

Dr. Miller took out his phone to photograph the book and the first page so that they would have a copy. He decided that the book needed to dry out some before they could handle the pages. Nokosa-bear pulled out an old ice chest he had in his storage closet to keep the book along with a container of DampRid to help dry it out. The product's simple container held white granules that wicked the extra moisture from the air and turned them into a salt solution, which was then trapped in a tray at the bottom of the container. Nokosa-bear put it in boats and lockers that were not opened often to remove the moisture that could cause mold.

Dr. Miller placed the log in the ice chest with the DampRid, then locked the chest in a large locker in the storage room so that it would be safe. Everyone said their good-byes and headed out for the night, agreeing that it would take a few days for the log pages to dry out.

The boys and Dr. Miller headed back to Everglade City and the motel, while Nokosa-bear checked on some boats in the marina before heading home himself. Dalton and Juan couldn't stop talking on their drive to the motel. Juan immediately pulled out his phone and called his parents to tell them about what they had found. From listening to the one side of the conversation, the Millers were glad they had brought Juan along this summer. As Juan talked on the phone, Dalton and Dr. Miller visited about what to do next.

"Dad, I think we should go back to Miami and see if there are any records about *El Dorado*," said Dalton. "Maybe we can find out where she was going and why just in case we are unable to read the log."

"You may be right, but I need to work on my reports tomorrow because I have to continue to prove my theories and justify my grant," said Dr. Miller. "While I'm doing that, you boys should spend the day playing around here either in the motel or go out and do some exploring. With the tide back in and the log drying, there are not a lot of things you can do except online research."

Dalton didn't want to hear that he and Juan couldn't go back out to the island and search, but he knew his dad was right. Between the tide and the time needed to dry out the pages, it didn't make sense. The scientist's son had become so focused on the find that he had forgotten about his father's own research.

When Juan got off of the phone, Dalton shared his father's thoughts with Juan. The teenage boys agreed to take a day off from their research and spend the next day helping Dr. Miller with his, but their minds were definitely on the log. So, the day was spent in the swamp, catch snails, dodging alligators and all the while thinking about their own find.

The following day, the boys woke up early, hoping that this would be the day that they were able to learn why the barrel and log were there and what happened to *El Dorado*. They made so much noise talking while eating breakfast that they woke Dr. Miller. He could not get upset with them since he was as curious as they were. Dr. Miller had purchased a Spanish-English dictionary when he went to Walmart the previous night, so they packed it along with a lunch and headed out to Chokoloskee Island and Nokosa-bear's marina. They did notice how strange it was that the two guys they had seen in the swamp earlier in the week were up also.

The chatter in the car ride was nonstop as if the car were filled with crows squawking.

"What do you think we will find in the log, Dr. Miller?" asked Juan.

"I don't know. But if the captain kept good records, we might learn who he was, where he was headed, and what cargo he was carrying," replied Dr. Miller.

Now the boys were really excited. They had talked about treasure before, but in the last few days they were focused on finding more clues. And then after finding the log, they became obsessed with translating it. They had not given a thought to what they might find in the ship if they found it, only that they might find a ship.

They arrived at the marina just as Nokosa-bear was finishing his morning rounds. He walked the marina every morning and every evening to look for damage or problems to the docks and the boats. The boat owners who moored their boats at his marina expected this service and knew that Nokosa-bear took it seriously, which is why his clients chose his marina. When Dr. Miller and the boys drove up, he greeted them warmly. He, too, was psyched about what they might learn today.

"Come on in. I was just heading in to put on some coffee," Nokosa-bear said, smiling at the two teenage boys. He remembered the adventures his relatives had put in his head when he was their age and now he was like one of them again, full of excitement. They went into the store, with the boys heading to the storage room while the men tended to the coffeepot—a sign of priorities of age—coffee or treasure.

The teenagers opened the locker but did not disturb the ice chest. They had been warned that the DampRid container would contain water and spilling it would mean another few days of waiting. While they were waiting for the "old men" to finish their coffees, Dalton gazed out the office window and saw the two men from the swamp who were staying at the motel. As the men got out of their car, Dalton again got that strange feeling that made the hairs on his arms stand up.

What was it about them that made him feel that way? he wondered.

Then he asked aloud, "Nokosa-bear, do you know the men who just drove up? Have you seen them before?"

Dalton pointed out through the blinds of the window at the two men as they got out of their car suspiciously looking around.

"I have never seen them before, why?" queried Nokosa-bear.

Looking out the window with the rest of them Dr. Miller said, "We have run into them now a couple of times, once in the swamp and another time at the motel."

The he told the Indian how Dalton got a funny feeling about being watched the other day on the sandbar, had experienced that feeling before when these men were present, and again the other day when they were out in the boat. Dr. Miller had checked but hadn't seen anyone.

"Dalton, are you getting that feeling again?" Dr. Miller asked his son.

"Yes, that is how I noticed them," Dalton said, shivering.

Nokosa-bear felt it was his responsibility to know who was on his property and what they needed. He was also the only one whom the two men had not seen already so he knew he could approach them without causing any suspicion. He walked out of the door, locking it behind him and headed their direction.

"You didn't tell me you were having these weird feelings, Dalton," said Juan.

"I know I felt embarrassed about them like I'm a scared little girl or something. I told my dad because I felt it again and we were alone. He had already noticed that I was acting strange," Dalton sheepishly replied.

"Dude, if I was having those feelings," said Juan, "I would tell my dad also, so don't worry, it's cool."

The boys and Dr. Miller listened as Nokosa-bear approached the men.

"How are you gentlemen today? Welcome to Chokoloskee Marina. What can I do for you?" asked Nokosa-bear.

"We were thinking about going out and wondered if you had a boat to rent?" the older looking of the two asked.

Thinking quickly, Nokosa-bear said, "I have a couple. My nicer and faster boat went out with a man and two boys in it earlier, but I have an older boat, if you don't mind."

The two men looked at each other and grinned.

"No, we don't mind. We thought we would go out and just see the area," said the younger-looking one. "It is so nice and peaceful out here. I bet you get a lot of people who want to just come out and ride around looking at the mangroves and the clear water like that father and boys who went out earlier."

Acting dumb, Nokosa-bear said, "Yes, we do get a lot of people who want to just go for a ride and see the scenery, but the other guys said they were out hunting snails in a bay north of here."

"That must be the doctor from Dallas who's staying at the same motel we are. We haven't met them yet, but the motel owner was telling us about them," added the older-looking man.

"That must be them. There are not a lot of places to stay out here so if you are at the Everglades Motel, I am sure it is. Come to think of it, he did say he was a professor studying snails in the area for the summer. I guess to each his own," Nokosa-bear snorted.

All of the men had a good laugh and walked out on a dock toward the boats. Nokosa-bear had one of them fill out a rental form he retrieved from a cabinet on the dock while he took the other man out to an older boat. The older boat was a small boat with a fifty-horsepower engine and dingy white paint. It looked like it was made about the same time that Nokosa-bear was born, but it was the only boat available. The old Seminole went over the instructions for operating the boat, the safety features, including life preservers and the limits as to how far they could take the boat out. It did not have ocean navigable safety items like a life raft, rations, or a GPS so he instructed them not to go out further than one quarter of a mile from land. Just as he was finishing the checklist of items to cover, the other man walked up with the papers in hand completed.

"Insurance requires a copy of your driver's licenses, so if you don't mind, I can just take pictures instead of going back to the store and copying them on the photocopier, if that is all right with you?" Nokosa-bear said to the men.

The two men allowed him to shoot a picture of their licenses, and Nokosa-bear helped by casting off the dock lines. The Seminole watched as they headed out of the marina and saw them as they turned north.

With a short snicker, Nokosa-bear headed back to the store.

"I just sent your buddies there on a wild goose chase north," said Nokosa-bear.

"What do you mean?" asked Juan.

"They have been watching you!" affirmed Nokosa-bear. "When I gave them a little information, they jumped right on it and told me they were staying in the same motel as you and they even asked which way you had gone. I told them you went north looking for a cove to hunt snails. We all laughed, but when they left the marina they headed north."

Dr. Miller pondered out loud, "So you were right, Dalton. These men must be tied to the one who claimed to be my brother when they spoke to your friend Chase. But who are they and how did anybody know what we are doing? We haven't told anyone."

"That scares me to know someone is following us," said Juan. "Do you think they know about the log and the possibility of treasure?"

"We know they suspect that we found something; otherwise, they would not have followed us," responded Dr. Miller.

"I did shoot photos of their driver's licenses during the rental," said Nokosa-bear. "We may be able to find out more about them. But there is one thing I know: they are going to be gone for a while searching for you up north. I suggest we continue with the opening of the log with one person keeping an eye on the window for their return.

He then told Dr. Miller to park his car down the road in the carport of a green-colored house owned by a friend who was not on the island this week. That way, if the men came back unexpectedly, they would think he had already left.

Dr. Miller agreed as he headed out the door and to the Jeep.

While Dr. Miller moved the car to the hidden location, the boys laid dry rags out to cover the table where they were going to decipher the log and turned on a fan that would gently cycle air through the room to dry any pages that were still damp. Nokosa-bear handed the boys latex gloves. With everyone ready, Nokosa-bear lifted the lid and carefully removed the DampRid container. He placed the chest on the table. Dr. Miller carefully reached into the chest with his gloved hands to pick up the log and put it on the rags. He grasped the leather binding and opened the log to the page they had previously read. Instead of Juan and Dr. Miller working on translating what was written, Dalton pulled out his phone and began to take photos of each page as his father turned them using a pair of tweezers from Nokosa-bear's medical kit. Sixty-three pages in the book had writing, Before Dalton took any photos, Dr. Miller gently dabbed dry the page and verified that it could be read. Once they had finished Dr. Miller wrapped the log again in the oilcloth and placed it in the office safe. This time, Nokosa-bear placed a DampRid container in the safe to remove any additional moisture, locked it, and then moved the printer table in front of the safe to hide it from plain view.

"How should we go about translating these pages? Should we start at the beginning and work forward, or start at the end and work backward?" Dalton queried as he flipped through the photographs he had taken.

"I say we start with the last entry and work backward, or try to skim to the beginning of his last voyage and work forward from there," replied Juan.

"If we can find the beginning of the last voyage, then that would be a way to at least see what we are looking for and where," suggested Dr. Miller. "We can always go to the beginning later to get a better picture of who the captain was and what the ship was like."

Then Dr. Miller asked Juan to translate the dates to get them to the last voyage. He thought Juan would find at least a larger gap between when the captain arrived in port and when he left or maybe just a long list that might be the cargo manifest or list of what they were carrying.

That seemed doable to Juan, so Dalton handed Juan the phone instead of sharing the pictures with him. After the encounter with the two men, they thought it would be best to have only one set of photographs on Dalton's phone until they could print them.

The last entry Juan found read "*10 de julio del 1502*"—July 10, 1502. As discussed, he did not stop to read, but continued swiping the screen to scroll through the pages until there seemed to be a break. It only took him three screens to get to a page labeled "*Santo Domingo, 1 de Julio del 1502*."

"It appears this is where they started the voyage from what I can tell. The days before July 1 were lists like you thought there would be, Dr. Miller," said Juan. "It looks to me like the voyage began in a place called Santo Domingo on July 1, 1502."

Nokosa-bear rushed over to a cabinet and returned with a nautical map. He spread it on the table where the log had been and then pointed to the Dominican Republic.

"Santo Domingo is the capital of the Dominican Republic," said the Seminole, "and was, if I remember my history, the main port for Spain in the Caribbean."

The place on the map, the date, and their previous research at the University of Miami's Marine and Atmospheric Library pointed directly to a hurricane that went through the Caribbean and specifically through the Dominican Republic in the beginning of July 1502. History and their logbook seemed to be lining up and telling the same story, a "true story."

Everyone shivered with excitement at the connection. They were now a part of history—and not just any history—something that happened more than five centuries ago!

In the midst of their elation, Dalton suddenly felt they were being watched. He immediately turned to look out the window and saw the two men from the motel getting out of the boat and onto the dock.

"They're back!" hollered Dalton, and everyone in the room first froze then turned to look out the window at the same time as if they were puppets on a string.

The mood in the room deflated, and no one spoke another word for almost a minute.

Nokosa-bear broke the silence and said, "Everyone needs to move to the storage room quickly. I will bring the two men into the office to finish their payment, and that will give them a chance to see that you are not hiding in here and hopefully not think that I am involved. If they do not suspect me, I can keep feeding them bad information as need be and learning what they know. It may be a way to always stay ahead of them."

Dr. Miller and the boys agreed, so they picked up everything that was theirs, including the Caribbean map. Then they headed to the storeroom and found boxes to sit on. Meanwhile, Nokosa-bear went to the front of the store, unlocked the door, and made himself to look busy.

As the two men opened the door to the marina office, Nokosa-bear picked up the phone and pretended to be talking to a friend about a boat. He smiled and waved, then held up one finger to indicate he would just be a minute more. It was a good cover for not meeting them out at the dock and it gave him a few minutes to observe them. They looked around a little and quietly talked about never finding the Millers.

"Their Jeep is gone also, maybe the Indian will know where they have gone," said Nick Barnes, the younger of the two men.

Ending his fake phone call, Nokosa-bear said, "We will get your boat in tomorrow and see if we can fix that prop for you."

Then he turned to the two men and said, "Sorry about that, gentlemen. One of my clients bent a prop on something floating, and he wants to use it again this weekend. How did the boat run for you?"

"It ran just fine," replied James Farmer, the older guy. "You were right. It is a little slow, but it made for an enjoyable sightseeing time. Can't very well see things when you are blowing past it like a rocket. By the way, is the other boat you rent out a lot faster than that one? Just thought I would ask in case next time we want to dash around these islands."

"Yah, it runs at about thirty-five knots whereas the one you guys had runs at about fifteen knots," laughed Nokosa-bear.

"Kind of the tortoise and the hare difference," quipped Farmer, which made everyone laugh.

"I didn't see another boat out there so I guess our motel neighbors haven't come back yet," interjected Barnes.

"Oh no, they came back about thirty minutes ago. I moved the boat over to a different dock since the tide is going out this evening," Nokosa-bear shared.

"I was surprised that they rented a boat considering they have one at the motel," Barnes asked, trying to pump information out of the Seminole.

"You know they did show up with a small boat a little while back," said Nokosa-bear. "But they said that they brought it for use in the swamp when the doctor was hunting snails there. They said after the first time out they thought a larger boat would be more comfortable out in the open waters. It worked for me. I made two hundred bucks along with gas money, so I'm not complaining. It kept them from having to stop and unhitch the boat before they went into the Walmart anyway. They said they had broken some nets, so they were in a rush to get them replaced."

"They must have found some pretty big snails then," remarked Barnes.

Quickly thinking, Nokosa-bear replied, "That would be funny if they had caught that big of a snail, but I heard the professor getting on to one of the boys for letting it get caught in the prop. Apparently chewed a hole right through it but didn't hurt the prop. The other boy was complaining about having to get in and cut the net loose from the prop."

Nokosa-bear would have to remember to tell Dalton and Juan his story so if asked they had the same answers.

Then Farmer walked up to the counter and Nokosa-bear handed him an invoice for $125. He slid his credit card through the machine and signed the receipt.

"My number is on the invoice in case you want to call ahead and reserve a boat next time," said Nokosa-bear.

Barnes thanked the Indian and also picked up one of his business cards.

"I have a feeling we will be back soon," he said as he and Farmer walked out the door.

Nokosa-bear watched the two men climb into their car and drive off toward the mainland. When the car was out of sight across the bridge, he went to the storage room to let Dr. Miller and the boys know that the coast was clear. He opened the door to find them staring at him wide-eyed as if they had been caught.

"They just left, so you guys are safe for now," said Nokosa-bear.

Dr. Miller and the boys collectively breathed a sigh of relief and then listened to the story Nokosa-bear had told Farmer and Barnes. They, too, wanted to make certain that their stories matched.

"I guess when we head back we will take the island's back road so that we appear to come from the east just in case they are watching," Dr. Miller decided. "It's also probably best to not discuss the log in the motel. If they have gone to these lengths to try to find out what we are doing, they may have bugged our room to hear what we know."

The boys sat there stunned. Someone was really watching them and trying to find out about what they had found.

"If we can't talk about it in our room, where can we work on translating the log and possibly finding more information?" Dalton impatiently asked.

"It looks like we are going to have to find other places and times to work on it," said Dr. Miller. "You boys could come back here on your bikes when I go to the swamp if I can get them to follow me. We may have to find places where we can go in the boat and work from there, we just have to be vigilant in knowing our surroundings and especially if Mr. Farmer and his mini me are anywhere around."

"You are always welcome to come here and work in my office, and I will help you all I can," added Nokosa-bear. That seemed agreeable to everyone.

Dalton and Juan decided to continue their work on the log. Nokosa-bear had a TV and an Apple TV connection that someone had left on a boat. The boys and their love for technology had Dalton's phone connected in no time to the TV, which gave everyone a view of the log's pages. Nokosa-bear's computer was a relatively new Dell with a pretty fast Internet connection, so they used it to research. They also had the Spanish/English dictionary Dr. Miller had bought and with their limited understanding of Spanish began to translate.

July 1, 1502

El Dorado *is loaded with cargo for Spain as are the other thirty-one caravels with their captains and crews. Each has seen to his load and his provisions, and after meeting the previous night, they have agreed to set sail with the tide this morning. The smaller caravels agree to try to sail in sight of the others for protection since their cargo was so valuable, the difficulty was the larger* El Dorado. *She carried more sails and should be able to keep up and even sail faster, but she has the heaviest cargo, so she would be the slowest. It was agreed that they would all keep pace with her. Each set sail to get out of the harbor and then slowed the pace to be able to stay together.*

Columbus had warned us not to leave, that a great storm was heading our direction, but the governor gave the orders to leave, and since he was the representative of His Majesty King Ferdinand II and Her Majesty Queen Isabella I, we agreed in spite of the warning. All ships are accounted for, and we are headed to catch the current and winds to clear the islands for our trip home. The eastern sky is filled with clouds, but the northeast seems to be clear so our heading was to steer northeast and skirt around the storm.

July 2, 1502

The storm seems to be larger than we anticipated. As we shifted northeast, it apparently did the same thing. The seas are rising and the waves roll out in front of it. The sailor on watch has reported seeing all of the other ships except the first three to leave port; they must be just out of view.

July 3, 1502

Because of the waves and the increased wind, we are struggling to clear the last of the islands. We hope to be able to pass them and in open waters soon to sail straight north. The wind is beginning to pound us, and we have shortened our sails to keep better control.

July 4, 1502

Poseidon the Greek god of the ocean must be angry with us because the wind and seas have risen so much that we have lost three sails. The boat is being tossed about like a rag doll. We are unable to see any of the other boats because of the darkness of the clouds and the amount of rain that is falling. Everyone is belowdecks except a few sailors to keep watch and tend to the boat.

July 5, 1502

We have not been able to take a star sighting for two days because the clouds and the rain have made it impossible to see anything. This has become the worst storm I have ever had to sail through, and the pounding is taking its toll on the crew. Those who are belowdecks are constantly baling water since it seems to be coming from every direction. The governor has become delirious with fear and causing some of my best sailors to doubt their abilities.

July 6, 1502

The storm has not let up and there seems to be no end in sight to it. More damage is being reported every hour as the storm acts as a battering ram against our wooden sides. One sailor said he spotted land during a flash of lightning, but that does not seem possible. We should have already cleared the islands. The rudder has broken loose, and we have lost the ability to control the ship.

July 7, 1502

The governor and a good part of the crew believe they have seen land and are asking to jettison the lifeboats to seek safety, knowing that we no longer have control of El Dorado. *My fear was made true when the crews in the lifeboats were almost immediately swamped and all sailors drowned, including the governor. Now with only two other crewmen left on the ship it seems all is lost.*

July 8, 1502

My crew has been washed off the ship, and I am now alone on a derelict ship with no way of knowing where I am and no end in sight to the storm. My only bearings have been the rising light and the occasional glimpses of land to the east of me, which must be the land that Columbus had charted north of Santo Domingo because it is large. I have fashioned a barrel with a rope as a flotation and have tied myself to it should I get swept off of the ship. I am sealing this log, wrapped to protect it, in the barrel so that I can have a record. My greatest fear now seems inevitable, my dear ship and all of its gold will be lost like my crew and most likely myself.

"That's the end of it, the last entry," proclaimed Juan.

The teenage boy was exhausted from translating and looking up unfamiliar words. Dr. Miller, Dalton, and Nokosa-bear sat quiet for a while as they took in the story. No one wanted to speak because they knew that these were the last words of a crew and faithful captain. Nokosa-bear quietly went over to his refrigerator and pulled out some Cokes, handing them out.

"I would like to toast this captain and his crew for their courage," Nokosa-bear reverently said, lifting his drink high in the air. "A toast to the crew of *El Dorado* and to Captain Antonio de Torres for their bravery and sacrifice. May their souls find peace."

It was a very solemn moment that touched everyone in the room.

"We read about things like these in social studies," Dalton said thoughtfully. "But they always seemed so far off not personal like this has become. I never felt this close to history before, now it seems as if we have to do something to give closure to this captain and crew."

"I was feeling the same way. I think we have an obligation to find out what we can and let the world know, like finishing the story in the history books," added Juan.

"Then it is settled. We will do our best to find answers and to give Captain de Torres the recognition he deserves," Dr. Miller added with admiration for his son and Juan.

"Let's get out the material we collected about the hurricane from the university library. Maybe we can get some clues as to where it went. Nokosa-bear, can we get your map again and layout what we know?" Dr. Miller inquired.

Nokosa-bear retrieved the map from the storeroom and laid it out on the table. Then he took out a grease pencil to mark the coordinates, the estimated direction, and speed. Juan pulled up hurricane tracking Web sites and began playing with estimates of where it would make landfall. He placed the locations that the

1502 hurricane was confirmed to hit and then added where they were. Most of the models had the storm curving back to land and not going out into the gulf again.

"If these plots are close to accurate, then the ship could have hit one of the sandbars and thrown the captain off with the barrel and continued on inland," said Dalton.

"From my experience, when they come this close to the western shore of Florida, they curve on across the land and die out," said Nokosa-bear. "So, I think if this is where we found the log, then the rest of the ship must be somewhere in the swamp."

"Why in the swamp? Why not out at sea?" queried Dalton.

"Well, if we found the log and barrel off of our shore along with the report of the man on the beach, it just seems logical that *El Dorado* went the same direction," replied Dr. Miller.

"So, Nokosa-bear, how do you think we should search the swamp and what do you think that we will be looking for?" asked Juan.

Nokosa-bear pondered this question for a while and then answered, "My first thought is that if it was close by, the Indians would have found it. But there is no report of them finding the ship. So, logic would tell us that it either sunk before it hit land, or the wind and waves drove it deep into the swamp, where it avoided detection."

"What might it look like today if we were to find it?" asked Juan.

"Why don't we Google and see if we can find what it might look like. Search for lost villages and other things that have taken hundreds of years to find, so we can get an idea of what we might be looking for," suggested Dr. Miller.

The boys began typing in straightforward questions: What would a five-hundred-year-old ship look like today? Old boats in ruins, old boats decaying on land? But none of which seemed to help them. They even looked at "tells," which are old towns or settlements, which had been abandoned in the Middle East. These tells created a cone-shaped mound, which might be true if a ship was forced on land in a normally flat area and left to decay.

"There is nothing that seems to match what we are looking for, but my research seems to say that if the area was flat then it might have created a mound that would be different from everything else around," Dalton commented after a long and unfruitful search.

"That would make sense because we know that the swamp is flat," said Nokosa-bear. "And in this area, it is more of a grass swamp, so anything sticking up might be conspicuous. We also know that it cannot be close to anything otherwise it would have already been noticed. So how do we find out if there is anything like this in the swamp since we cannot search the whole thing?"

"Satellite maps!" yelled Dalton. "Juan, you know how we played on Google Maps looking at our homes and the homes of our friends. They were created by a car driving down the street, but we could also see an overview, which had to have been done by an airplane or satellite."

Dalton began to type these search words on the keyboard.

"What if we just look for images of this area of the swamp and see if there is anything unusual?" Dalton suggested.

He keyed southwest Florida into Google Maps as Dr. Miller, Juan, and Nokosa-bear stood around the monitor. Since Nokosa-bear knew the area better than the rest of them, he gave Dalton directions and described what they were looking at on the screen. He helped them create a systematic search of the swamp. Every time they came to something unusual, they stopped and focused in closer. Most of the time, it was a larger bush, but after about an hour and a half they had identified five areas that looked like mounds, which were not on main waterways. They printed out maps and marked each of the spots to personally examine.

It was getting late, and they still needed to make their fake trip to Walmart. Nokosa-bear agreed to take the boys into the swamp the next day while Dr. Miller would draw the guys back north. Nokosa-bear locked up the marina and prepared to make his evening rounds as Dr. Miller and the teenage boys walked down to where the Jeep was parked and headed back to the mainland.

Chapter 11

Swamp Search

The next morning, Juan and the Millers decided to eat breakfast at the diner. It was just a couple of blocks away, so they walked in the cool morning air. Putting on the appearance of normality was the idea; they did not make a big show of leaving. But at some point, Juan, Dalton, and Dr. Miller each looked toward the motel room occupied by James Farmer and Nick Barnes to see if they were watching. The drapes were slightly parted, so it was hard to tell. But Dalton continued having that feeling that they were being observed. Breakfast out was great because the boys got to eat more than cereal or powdered doughnuts. Today, it was a big breakfast day with bacon, scrambled eggs, biscuits, and hash browns. What more could a teenager want except more of the same in larger quantities. They laughed and ate, but Dalton felt and then saw through the diner's window that one of the two men was watching them. He wondered, *Did we mess up their breakfast by us getting up early and going out to eat?* But he did not feel sorry for them. They were the ones following us, so the more uncomfortable they were the better, according to Dalton.

After extra biscuits and juice, Dr. Miller paid the bill, left a good tip, and he and the boys walked back down to the motel.

When the three of them got back to the motel, Dr. Miller connected the boat trailer to the Jeep, loading all of the equipment and buckets they used to collect snail samples. They did not do it quietly. They wanted to make certain that their shadows knew exactly what they were going to do. Once loaded, they leisurely drove out to the island. For what they had planned, they wanted an audience; otherwise, it would not be as much fun. With both Millers in the front seat of the Jeep, it was Juan's job to see if they were being tailed. Sure enough, just as they were crossing the bridge, he caught site of a car slowly following them. When they arrived at the marina, the boys jumped out of the car and readied the boat. In the meantime, Dr. Miller greeted Nokosa-bear, who had just finished his morning rounds.

As soon as the boat was ready to launch, the boys crawled into it and Dr. Miller backed it down the ramp. Dalton started the boat's engine and backed the boat off of the trailer and close to the dock. After Dr. Miller parked the Jeep and trailer in the lot, he climbed onboard the boat and took over the wheel. Still on watch, Juan saw that the two men had parked just on the edge of the bridge to keep from being noticed. As soon as Dalton and Juan were seated, Dalton's father pulled the boat away from the dock and headed out.

James Farmer and Nick Barnes waited for the boat to round the dock before they drove down to the marina and flagged Nokosa-bear down.

"We would like to rent a boat again if you have one available," said Farmer.

Laughing, Nokosa-bear said, "Didn't get enough yesterday? The water is like that; once you get a taste of it, you seem to want to get back out ASAP."

"Something like that," Barnes snorted.

Knowing that the two men were in a hurry, Nokosa-bear fumbled around with the paperwork and keys trying to give Dr. Miller, Dalton, and Juan a head start, but not trying to make it obvious he was stalling. Farmer and Barnes waited impatiently for the rental transaction to be completed while the younger man kept an eye out for which direction Dr. Miller was headed. Just as Nokosa-bear was finishing the paperwork and handing them the keys, the two men saw the other boat turn north up the Intracoastal Waterway like they believed Dr. Miller had done the day before. They did their best to catch up but followed at a distance, so that they would not be noticed.

Watching the whole thing happen from the dock, Nokosa-bear walked back to the store, closed the door, and headed to an airboat at the end of the docks, owned by a friend. Nokosa-bear did so much work for the friend that he allowed him to use it whenever it was needed. This monster of a boat had a flat bottom about twenty feet long with an up-raked bow and a huge airplane propeller and engine on the back that stood about eight feet high. The hull of the boat was painted green and tan with what looked like scales drawn into the design. Written in large black letters was the boat's name, *The Snake*, with the letter *S* looking like a cobra. The owner said his airboat didn't move through the swamp like a normal boat, it slithered, hence the name. Sitting in the lower two seats just above water level were Dalton and Juan. Nokosa-bear was sitting a tier higher, so he could see over everyone else to steer the boat.

"You guys didn't have any trouble getting off your dad's boat and onto the dock when he passed, did you?" the Seminole asked the boys.

"No," replied Dalton. "It was actually kind of fun pulling a James Bond move on those guys. As soon as we turned down the side of all of the docks, the other boats kept us out of sight, so Dad slowed down, and we jumped onto the dock as he sped off. He didn't even have to come to a complete stop."

"Yah, I think if you had been standing close you would not have seen us get off we were so slick," offered Juan. "Maybe we should start doing magic tricks. Now you see us, now you don't."

"Just remember, this is fun for you, but for those two guys it is serious business; otherwise, they would not be out here following you," warned Nokosa-bear.

Then the Seminole started the huge engine as Juan pulled out the aerial photographs they had printed from Google Earth and Dalton untied the dock lines. Revving the engine, they took off the opposite direction, curved under the road bridge with just a few feet of clearance, and headed back into the swamp to try and find their first mound. The adrenaline rush of the airboat was great, but the real excitement was the thought that they might find *El Dorado* in one of the mounds they had marked to investigate.

Nokosa-bear had been in and around the swamp all his life, so he knew his way around the main arteries. But because storms and rain changed the streams leading off of the main bayou, they had to rely on the aerial photograph to guide them. Juan took pictures of landmarks like trees, different grass formations, and anything else that could help them find their way out in case they got lost. They couldn't very well leave bread crumbs like Hansel and Gretel—something would have definitely eaten them.

They followed their plan and arrived at the first area to search, an area with high reeds along the bank and some kind of mound a little farther inland.

"Boys, your dad told me you bought knives after your first trip into the swamp," said Nokosa-bear. "He also instructed you on how to be careful. It goes without saying that you need to have your weapons handy because everything here wants to eat something, and two boys would make a great meal."

The old Seminole did not laugh when he said it. Even with his great sense of humor, he was taking their safety seriously because he knew how dangerous the swamp could be and he had grown fond of these two teenagers, treating them like they were his own grandsons. As he was sliding the boat up to the shoreline, he reached around to a holster on the side of his seat, which carried a twelve-gauge shotgun and then he pulled a pistol and holster out of a box under his seat. Dalton and Juan had not given it a thought as Dr. Miller had carried his pistol out into the swamp with them. As a precaution, Nokosa-bear fired off the shotgun at the shoreline shredding the willows that stood on the water's edge.

"I don't like to get bit and they don't like to get shot, so I let them know my intentions and they seem to stay out of my way," Nokosa-bear said as he snorted over the ringing of the gun blast in the boys' ears.

Dalton and Juan watched as all sorts of birds squawked and flew off in every direction not wanting to be near another gun blast. As the boat pulled up onshore, Nokosa-bear handed each boy a machete to hack at the grass to clear a path and to hack at anything that bites.

"Remember watching the pirates trudge onto the shore in *Pirates of the Caribbean: The Curse of the Black Pearl?* I kind of feel like we are them, only we are the good guys," said Juan.

"Please don't make that mean that I am Captain Jack Sparrow. He was a weird dude," joked Nokosa bear.

Everyone had a good laugh and began to tease the old Seminole. Juan asked him to imitate Johnny Depp's funny faces in the movie. But the pirates who were chasing them—Farmer and Barnes—were chasing their decoy, Dr. Miller.

Dalton and Juan continued hacking away at grass and poking around with their sticks as they moved toward the area they had marked on the map. The ground began to rise, and the vegetation around the area became very dark and dense. They realized that they had walked up on the mound they had marked to find.

Nokosa-bear, Dalton, and Juan stood there for a minute trying to figure out the best way to attack this clump of vegetation. Juan started swinging his machete in the thick reeds and grass as everyone else followed suit. But instead of being relatively flat, there seemed to be a huge hump. Nokosa-bear and Dalton tried to clear some growth at the top of the mound but still couldn't figure out what was creating its height. Finally, Dalton found an area that seemed to be less dense, so he began to chop away, swinging the machete one direction and then turning his wrist and swinging it back the other. Before long, he had created a hole. Then Nokosa-bear and Juan joined in to help make the hole bigger.

"Freeze!" shouted Juan at Dalton. "Don't move."

Dalton stopped abruptly and looked at Juan with huge eyes with a look of "What!" on his face. Juan swung his machete straight down into the tall grass almost hitting Dalton's feet. Lying in two halves underneath his blade was a water moccasin, a deadly black snake that had been sunning itself in the tall grass.

"That was close. I'm glad you saw it; otherwise, I would have stepped right on him and gotten bit," sighed Dalton. "How did you kill it so quickly?"

"When I visit my grandparents in Mexico, we always have to be on the lookout for snakes. That's the not the first snake I have hacked to death," laughed Juan.

"Well, I hope for our sake, it's the last one you have to hack up!" bellowed Dalton.

Flicking the two pieces of the body of the snake out of the way with the tip of his machete, Juan stepped in closer and thought he saw something.

"Whatever is in there is blue and white and looks like a boat," he told Dalton and Nokosa-bear.

"Are you sure, Juan, you're not just pulling my leg since I'm already scared from the snake?" asked Dalton, a little put out from what he thought was a joke.

"No, he's right. It is a wooden boat, but it's not the boat we are looking for," said Nokosa-bear. "This one looks more like it was built in the 1950s. There was a hurricane that blew through in the early sixties that carried off a number of boats. This one was probably carried up here by the wind and storm surge and then hidden from the owners and insurance adjusters who went out looking for it."

"It's not going to surprise me then if we find more of these stuck out here too far away for most people to search," said Dalton. "Plus, they didn't have Google satellite maps to guide them."

"Well, I guess that means we can cross this site off of our list," said Juan.

With that, the boys and the Seminole turned around and trudged back to the airboat, planning their route to the next sight.

"How could you lose a boat in swamp like the one we just found?" Dalton asked Nokosa-bear.

"It's really pretty simple," replied Nokosa-bear. "If the storm is very large, the boat can be pushed so far in that no one would think to look this deep in the swamp. They usually just think it was carried back out to sea in the storm and destroyed. Many get so battered by the waves that they are crushed, with pieces deposited here and there, making it even harder to find."

Then a discussion began about *El Dorado*. The boys assumed the ship had been pushed inland because of where Juan found the barrel and the reports of the dead man on the beach. She could be lying anywhere from the swamps to back out in the deep water of the Gulf of Mexico.

"There is a good chance we are just wasting our time out here looking in the swamp," Nokosa-bear said, not meaning to discourage the boys but trying to just be honest with them.

But Juan said with a grin on his face, "This is too exciting to be wasting our time. If we were at home, we would be inside playing video games or out playing soccer. This summer, we have done more than that, we have been chasing snails with Dr. Miller, researching a lost ship, and almost getting eaten by snakes and alligators. At least this is something that we have never done before."

Juan then told the Seminole how much he enjoyed hanging out with him, listening to the way he talked about the history of this place, and about growing up here as a boy with all of those tales.

"How could a boy not love this?" Juan said emphatically.

"It does make me feel like a kid again running around in the swamp with you two chasing treasure," Nokosa-bear remarked. "At my age, it could be the last real fun I have, so let's go chase some more mounds!"

Crawling back into the boat, the old Seminole and the teenage boys headed back to the main artery of water. They kept going farther south until they saw a double fork in the stream. Checking their aerial map, they chose to venture down the third stream on the left. Juan took pictures to use as landmarks, including a brownish spot of grass that looked like it had been burned in the past. Nokosa-bear explained that it could have easily been made by a lightning strike that was quickly put out by the rain, something neither of the boys had ever thought about before.

This particular stream seemed to go farther back into the swamp than the other ones and was a little wider than most. According to the aerial photograph, if they followed the stream until it took a sharp curve left, they would reach a smaller stream and then have to turn right. They didn't need to get out to search for this mound. It was very obvious from the shore. As they got closer to their destination, Nokosa-bear fired his shotgun again to scare off any alligators. This time, he and the boys heard several splashes as the huge beasts rushed underwater. Everyone became a little more nervous knowing that there were definitely alligators in the area.

As the boat slid up on the shore, Dalton scanned the grass and began probing it with his stick. He was not going to be surprised by a deaf alligator that was hungry. Convinced that he was safe for the moment, he stepped out, swinging the machete to and fro to cut down the grass and taller plants. Since the boys and Nokosa-bear could see the mound clearly, they headed in that direction with Dalton in the lead, Nokosa-bear in the middle with the shotgun, and Juan bring up the rear, making certain no alligators came back.

The mound seemed to be taller than the last, towering over their heads by seven or eight feet. There were vines and grass growing up the side of it so they decided to stay together and work in a central location to keep an eye out for anything hungrier than they were. After what they had heard, no one wanted to be alone in this place, including Nokosa-bear.

"You boys start chopping in that area to the right," ordered Nokosa-bear. "I will be just behind you, keeping an eye out with the gun. If you see anything dangerous, scream and I will turn your direction. Don't move unless I tell you to; so if I have to shoot, you will not run directly into my line of fire."

A little shocked at the thought, both boys agreed that seemed the safest way to work.

"Let's set up a safe distance between us. Stretch out the arm holding the machete toward me and I will do the same," suggested Juan to Dalton. "This way, we can use our machetes to protect us from animals, but be far enough away. I don't want you to hit me just to keep me from beating you on the soccer field, okay?"

Dalton gave his friend one of those "yeah, right" looks and then stretched out his arm holding the machete. "I guess it works both ways, Juan," Dalton chuckled.

The undergrowth was very dense. And even though the machetes were sharp, the boys had to use a lot of strength to clear it away. Breathing hard and sweating like an Eskimo in a sauna, the boys continued hacking. Nokosa-bear left the machete work to the boys, even though he was in good shape for his age. He watched with a careful eye the area in front of them and also all around them for any sign of danger. The boys continued to swing their machetes and rake away the cut vegetation. After about thirty minutes, the teenage boys took a break. Standing there, panting with sweat covering their bodies as if it had been raining, they surveyed what they had done. They had cut a path about fifteen yards long and five yards wide into the thicket. Lawn mowers they were not, but at least now they could easily see and walk around the area.

"I can't believe we haven't reached something yet," said Juan. "We found the other boat in a matter of a few minutes."

"That could be a good sign," said Dalton. "This is thicker, which could mean it has been here longer. If it took us ten minutes to cut through sixty years of brush, how long do you think it will take us to get through five hundred years of undergrowth?"

Everyone agreed Dalton had made a great point: more work meant that it had been here longer. The boys passed around a bottle of water and after ten minutes went back to work. All the time, Nokosa-bear had been poking around the edges of the area they had just cut. He was both searching for an opening and making certain that something was not lying in wait to take a bite out of them. Though he tried, he could not see anything dangerous or any signs of what had made the mound.

As Dalton and Juan flailed their machetes back and forth, they talked about soccer, video games, and other things Nokosa-bear knew very little about. They even talked about girls in school that each of them liked. At least that was a subject Nokosa-bear understood. The boys both got into a rhythm with their swings. The motion resembled a pendulum with blades swinging left and right the same distance, creating a large arc. They did not know that they were even doing it until Nokosa-bear pointed it out. They realized they had covered more ground working together than they had working separately as if they were one large lawn mower. They continued swinging in unison, saying "left, then right, then left then right" and were able to clear another twenty yards in about fifteen minutes.

All of a sudden, Juan's foot hit something that wasn't dirt.

"I'm standing on something!" shouted Juan.

Nokosa-bear and Dalton immediately stopped what they were doing. Probing around Juan's foot with his machete, Dalton discovered that Juan was standing on a board. Having learned that storms and water moved things around the swamp all the time, there was no telling what could have been washed up over the years. They began scraping away the grass and dirt and were surprised to find a board that was three inches thick and about ten feet long.

"Do you think this could be part of the ship?" Juan asked.

No one could really answer that question because it could have come from anywhere.

"Let's hope it is something and keep clearing this area," answered Dalton. The boys continued their work with renewed vigor.

They returned to their swinging motion of back and forth. After about thirty more minutes, Dalton's machete got stuck in something that wrenched his hand at the same time.

"Owwwww!" Dalton screamed as he shook his right hand and pointed to his machete. "My hand has gone numb. I can't feel anything except that jarring feeling vibrating up my arm. Look, my machete is stuck and just sticking out of the brush like someone was holding it."

Juan and Nokosa-bear focused on Dalton's finger pointing to the handle of his machete sticking out of the brush. Nokosa-bear walked over to retrieve the machete and examine the area.

"Dalton, you hit a huge piece of wood," Nokosa-bear exclaimed. "No wonder your hand is hurting and your machete got stuck."

Juan drew in close and carefully began clearing away the brush around the piece of wood, making certain not to strike it with his machete. Then he found another wooden board sticking up out of the ground, even larger than the one Dalton had struck with his machete. Its curved shape seemed like a finger reaching up to the sky.

Juan continued clearing the area. He found more boards that curved upward and were evenly spaced, like a dinosaur rib cage lying on its back.

"I think this is a ship," Dalton said with excitement.

Dalton's hand felt better so he began hacking again, clearing away the grass and vines. Both he and Juan continued to find more wood and soon realized they were walking on wooden boards.

"I thought a ship would be taller," Dalton exclaimed.

"Most of it looks like it's buried in the ground. Like it had settled there and everything began to pile up around it," Nokosa-bear surmised.

If his guess was right, the boys and the Seminole were standing on the deck of a five-hundred-year-old ship. Much of it had most likely decayed and or had been washed away during storms, but there was still more underneath their feet.

The boys continued to work, clearing away the brush, finding more and more of the ship. Most of the vegetation seemed to be outside of what they thought was the hull. The work seemed easier. Perhaps it was because they knew that they were actually clearing away brush from a ship. It was not until the upturned wood came to an abrupt stop at about ninety feet when they got a real idea how large the ship was originally. They had worked for hours without stopping and without even realizing how late it was. The adrenaline drove them to work harder and longer than the two teenage boys had ever worked in their lives. When they reached the stern of the boat and they had the top of the hull cleared, they stopped and caught their breath. Nokosa-bear looked down at his watch and saw how late it was getting.

"Juan, take pictures of everything," Nokosa-bear directed. "We are going to have to cover the front of the hull with some brush so it can't not be seen and come back to search some more. We cannot stay any longer because it will get dark soon and you do not want to be in the swamp after dark. Then the animals have all of the advantages, and we cannot see clearly where we are going."

Juan took out his phone and took pictures of what they had uncovered. As soon as Juan had shot a portion of the hull, Dalton covered the front of the ship with brush and vines. It seemed almost a shame after so much work to do so, but they had to be careful.

Uncovering it would be a breeze compared to all the cutting they had done to clear it. When they were finished, they collected all of their tools and headed back to the airboat.

"What if someone finds it?" Juan asked.

"It's going to be dark in about four hours so even if they do they will not have time to do anything here. We don't want to leave any traces that we have been here, so let's mess up the grass where we walked on the way out and shove off," ordered Nokosa-bear.

Disappointed they had to leave, the boys did as they were told knowing that the old Seminole was right. The also knew that they had to get back to the marina to help cover their tracks with Dr. Miller and the guys following them. If Dr. Miller showed up at the marina and the boys were not around, then that would send up a red flag to their shadows.

Using the map and Nokosa bear's keen sense of direction, the three of them wound their way back through the swamp as fast as they could toward the marina. The old Seminole decided to beach the airboat just on the other side of the island and they would walk back to his office.

"We do not need to make the two men any more suspicious than they already are," said Nokosa-bear to the boys, "so beaching the boat here leaves us a short walk, which would be easier to explain than us showing up in a boat built for the swamp."

He then asked Dalton to call his father to find out where he was so they would know how to approach the area. Luckily, Dr. Miller was on his way back to the marina. In fact, in a few minutes he would be turning the corner that led straight in, so Dalton and Juan rushed back to the buildings by the marina just in time to see Dalton's father nearing the dock.

"Quick, head back to the dock and slide back into the boat like we got off," Dalton directed Juan.

Dr. Miller saw the boys immediately and knew what they had planned. He swung by the dock and slowed just enough for Dalton and Juan to jump in. Dr. Miller turned the boat back out away from the dock hoping that the two guys who had been following him from a distance would see the boys with him when they came around the corner. He made a big circle and then slowed down to head in. They all began to wave at Nokosa-bear, who was standing up by the office door. He had crossed the island but not at the speed of fourteen-year-old boys, and he was glad to see that they had reversed what they had done that morning by getting back into the boat. Over their shoulders, the other boat seemed to languish, waiting for them to dock and hitch their boat to the trailer. Dalton pulled the boat to the dock and let his father retrieve the Jeep and trailer, then slowly drove the boat up until it was resting firmly in the trailer's cradle. Dr. Miller pulled the Jeep up with the boys still in the boat and moved to the parking lot as if he had rewound them launching the boat this morning.

"Dalton, fill your father in about our day then call me tonight, so we can make plans," Nokosa-bear said before quickly walking away, making it look like he had just greeted his customers but was not overly interested it what they had been up to.

The boys finished cinching down the straps that held the boat on the trailer and then got in the Jeep and Dr. Miller pulled away. They could hardly contain themselves trying to tell Dr. Miller what they had found. He immediately put his hand up to quiet them. He was very interested in what they did, but at the moment he need to concentrate on two things at once, and their noise made it difficult. They stopped talking as soon as they realized what he was doing. He was driving forward, but his eyes were in the mirror watching the other boat pull up to the dock. He slowed as he crossed the bridge to see the two men from the motel get out of their boat; all the while he kept a very serious look on his face.

After a few moments of intense silence, he said, "Guys, I hope you found something because avoiding those two men and trying to make certain they did not get close enough to see you were missing was a challenge. I had to move every time I thought they were getting close and talk to myself as if I was talking to you guys; so that if they heard anything, they would think you were with me."

The boys had not given any thought as to what Dr. Miller had been doing. They were so wrapped up in their work they failed to think about the danger that he had been in all day. It was a sobering thought.

As soon as they cleared the bridge, Dr. Miller said, "Okay, tell me about your day and why we need to make more plans."

Dalton took the lead in telling his dad what he and Juan had dug up today since he was the one who found the first piece of the ship's frame, including the snake.

He began to describe how they had searched the first spot, then came to the second and began clearing it. Once he hit the piece of wood, the teenage boys began clearing the area and found the upward curving posts that seemed to be part of the ship's frame. They continued working until they found the whole deck of the ship, which was around ninety feet long. He told his father that Nokosa-bear thought the boat had sunk into the ground or the ground had covered up most of the ship over the years. When the boys and the Seminole realized how late it was, they camouflaged the ship with brush and vines so that it would not be easily seen from the water.

Excited and out of breath, Dalton said, "Dad, we have to go back and clear it out to see whether it is *El Dorado* or not! We only know that it is a ship, but we didn't find anything that would tell us which ship or how old it was. That's the reason we must go back tomorrow if possible. We can't let someone else find it."

With that, both boys collapsed into their seats, realizing this was the first time they had sat down all day.

Dr. Miller drove back to the motel in contemplative thought. The teenage boys and Nokosa-bear had potentially found not only an important part of history but possibly a very valuable treasure. All that was very exciting, but there were two men who seemed to be following them. And if there was any treasure, then this could become very dangerous for all of them, especially if James Farmer and Nick Barnes attempted to claim the treasure. Both men were large, and even though they had not made any physical threats, they did appear to Dr.

Miller to be accustomed to using force if necessary. In his mind, he was weighing whether all of this was worth placing Dalton and Juan in danger. There was nothing more valuable to him than his son and for that matter, Juan also, so he was hesitant to consider anything he thought might put them at risk.

Nokosa-bear had just finished his final rounds of the marina when his office phone rang. Dr. Miller was on the other end of the line.

"Nokosa-bear, the boys told me about the discovery today," said Dr. Miller. "Do you think that this could be what we were searching for?"

"So far, all we know is that it was a wooden ship somewhere around ninety feet long," said Nokosa-bear. "It looks like it has been there for a while and that much of the ship has been buried by silt and dirt over the years. I can't tell you if it is *El Dorado* until we find something that clearly says it is. But whatever it is, I think we need to look at it closer."

"What do you think about the two guys that have been following us? Do you think that they could be a danger to all of us?" asked Dr. Miller.

Considering the question over in his mind, Nokosa-bear replied, "Yes, I think James Farmer and that younger guy with him, Nick Barnes, potentially could present a danger to us."

"So, do we continue on with our search or do we go to the authorities and let them do something about it?" Dr. Miller asked with great apprehension in his voice.

"Today, we fooled them, but it is going to be harder each time we go out," replied Nokosa-bear. "I don't believe they are the kind of guys you can pull the wool over their eyes, at least for very long. Though I think we need to verify in some way that the ship is *El Dorado*, I do not want to put us at risk.

The Seminole then explained to Dr. Miller that they needed to find a way to authenticate the ship's identity and then contact professionals who could excavate the site and preserve its history. Nokosa-bear was as excited about the find as the boys were, but he also knew that he was more at home in the swamp than Farmer and Barnes, the two men who were following them.

"I was thinking the same thing but still very concerned for our safety," said Dr. Miller. "Let's set up one more run out there, all four of us, and do some light probing for anything to date."

After thinking for a moment, Nokosa-bear came up with a plan.

"I have a metal detector that we could take and some shovels," said Nokosa-bear. "I will load them into the airboat and we will meet …"

Chapter 12

Deception and Digging

When Dr. Miller and the boys arrived back at the motel, they made a phone call to help them set up an alibi or a deceptive cover to the plan suggested to them by Nokosa-bear. Mr. Langston was watering the plants out front when they arrived, just as they had planned. They knew that the men tailing them would be a few minutes behind them, so they slowed down and even stopped at a bait shop to pick up a drink so their tail could catch up and, in this case, pass them.

James Farmer and Nick Barnes were just getting out of their vehicle when the Jeep pulled up and the boys spilled out of it. They all waved at Mr. Langston hollered a loud "Hello."

Acting anxious to get inside but still speak to the motel owner, Dr. Miller greeted him in loud voice, "How are you today, Mr. Langston?"

"Well, thank you. How is the snail hunting going? Are y'all chasing them down?" laughed Mr. Langston.

Everyone got a good laugh at that, including Dr. Miller who had for years been kidded about his work by people who were not in his field. He didn't mind because most people did not know the importance the snail has on the local ecosystem. They only know that snails are slow and will dehydrate or melt when salt is poured on them.

"We are going to be in Fort Myers for a day or two starting tomorrow," Dr. Miller told Mr. Langston. "One of my colleagues has shipped me some new equipment, and it needs to be picked up. It would be great if you could keep an eye on the boat for us."

"Sure," replied Mr. Langston. "While you're there, would you pick up something for me? I've been in need of a new power washer and my supplier is there. I can give you the address and have it ready so it will not slow y'all down if you think you have room."

"We would be happy to do that for you," said Dr. Miller. "Just text me the address."

Then Dr. Miller and the boys went inside; all the while James Farmer and Nick Barnes had been languishing around their car listening, just as everyone had hoped.

"Do you think that we should follow them into Fort Meyers?" asked Barnes.

"Mr. Lanning told us to follow them and find out if they have found anything about the ships that were wrecked," replied Farmer. "We will have to be very careful because if they see us up there they will know that we are following them."

"I'll put a homing device on their car, so we can track them at a distance that will keep us from being seen," said Barnes.

"How big is that bug you're going to plant?" asked Farmer.

"It's smaller than a lapel button. Why?" said Barnes.

"The Spanish boy left his backpack in the car, and he has been carrying it around everywhere he goes," said Farmer. "You can slip it in there so when they get to Fort Myers, we may even be able to track where they are walking."

"Great idea!" said Barnes.

The younger man slipped into their room and came back out a second later apparently with the tracking device. As Farmer slowly walked past Room 5, Barnes slipped into the car and tucked it under the zipper of Juan's backpack. With more confidence in being able to keep track of Dr. Miller and the boys, the two men headed to the diner to eat because neither of them could cook.

After finishing their meal, they headed back to the motel and saw the Jeep was still there so they headed off to bed early, not knowing what time Dr. Miller and the two teenagers were going to leave.

The deception began early the next day. Sticking with their story, Dr. Miller, Dalton, and Juan crawled into the Jeep at about seven in the morning and headed out. Farmer had been standing watch near the window when Dr. Miller and the boys got into their Jeep. He had been standing back from the curtain so that he could not be seen through the small slit he had opened between the curtains to have a clear view of their car. He had been up since five, just in case they left early and had eaten some toast and was drinking coffee on a stool when he saw them drive off.

"Okay, let's go," Farmer said to his partner. "They are getting into their car now. We will give them a minute and then follow."

As Farmer and Barnes stepped out of their room, Mr. Langston was out sweeping up the drive, a job he typically did early in the morning when it was cooler.

"Good morning, gentlemen. Sleep well?" he asked.

"At my age, I rarely sleep well, but—" replied Farmer, pointing his thumb over his shoulder at the younger Barnes, "he sleeps like a rock."

"I know what you mean," said Mr. Langston, chuckling. "The older I have gotten the less I seem to sleep. Wait till you get my age and you will be forced to take a short nap because you didn't sleep that long the night before. Have you enjoyed the swamp so far?"

As he got ready to get in the car, Barnes replied, "It's not like all of the pictures and programs on TV. It seems much more primeval with the gators and such."

"I'm sure it does. You boys going back out in it today?" Mr. Langston asked.

"Not today. We need to run into Walmart," answered Farmer. "It seems I need some rubber boots, and then we thought about heading farther south to see what is that direction."

"Well, have a good trip," Mr. Langston replied, and waved as the two men got into their car and drove off.

Immediately, Mr. Langston walked into the office and called Dr. Miller's cell phone as they had discussed the previous afternoon.

"Farmer and Barnes just left the motel," said Mr. Langston. "I tried to stall them a little for you. When you called me yesterday and told me about them following y'all at first, I did not believe it. But the more I thought about it, they did seem to come and go about the same time you did. When I saw them come out the door just as y'all pulled off, I knew for certain that's what they were doing."

The motel owner then offered to report the men to the local sheriff. He told Dr. Miller that he and the sheriff had been friends for years and that he was a very respected law officer. He knew the sheriff would believe him if he described what had been going on and that the authorities would keep Farmer and Barnes under surveillance.

Dr. Miller thanked Mr. Langston for his offer.

"I know it seems weird to us, too," he told the motel owner. "If you want to call him and fill him in, that would be great. I am not sure that there is anything that can be done, but at least the authorities will know. Make certain that you tell them Nokosa-bear has been working with us since he and the sheriff are probably friends as well."

"I will and be safe," warned Mr. Langston as he hung up the phone.

True to his word, the motel owner immediately dialed the sheriff's personal cell phone number. Since they had been friends almost all their lives, he knew the sheriff was up and probably having breakfast. When the sheriff answered, Mr. Langston explained what was going on, the sheriff agreed to keep an eye on Farmer and Barnes.

As Dr. Miller finished the phone call, Dalton was pointing to a small dirt side road that led back out into the swamp. Nokosa-bear had told them exactly where to turn off of the main road. The dirt road curled back to the right and came up along the bayou where there was a worn-down area that had been used by fishermen as a parking area. They pulled over, drove down the road, and sure enough, Nokosa-bear was waiting there for them in the airboat.

"Good morning," the Seminole said. "Quick, get in and let's shove off so we can have as much daylight as possible."

As the boys got out of the car, Dalton handed Juan several bottles of water. "Can you carry these for us?"

"Sure," Juan said, taking them.

It made more sense to put the water bottles in his backpack so he could have his hands free, so Juan slipped them into it and then threw the pack over his shoulder as he headed toward the boat with the others. Little did he know that it contained the tracking device planted by Nick Barnes.

"Did they take the bait?" Nokosa-bear asked Dr. Miller.

"Yes," said Dr. Miller. "Mr. Langston telephoned us to say he visited with them a few minutes to delay them, so we could turn off the road without being seen."

Dr. Miller and the boys waited a couple of minutes to listen to see if a car went down the highway, and sure enough it did. They were far enough away to not be seen but close enough to hear the hum of the tires on the asphalt road.

"That sounds like they headed toward town, and they did not stop. Let's go see this boat you guys found," said Dr. Miller, excited to be a part of the group again instead of being the one in charge of distraction.

Dr. Miller and the boys climbed into the boat and Nokosa-bear started it up. He swung the air boat into the bayou and headed out into the swamp to pick up the streams that led to their find. Between the map and Juan's pictures, they were able to steer to the correct finger of the waterway and pull up in the same spot they had pulled up the day before.

While Dr. Miller, Nokosa-bear, and the boys were preparing to slip away in the swamp boat, James Farmer and Nick Barnes were pulling away from the motel, in hopes of catching up.

"How does that tracking device work?" Farmer asked his partner, knowing that technology was not his strength.

"It is really pretty simple," said Barnes as he switched on the device. "The tracker sends out a signal that I can see on this GPS. Even though it's small, the same satellite that the GPS uses picks up the bug and then shows me where they are."

It took a minute for a blue arrow to register where Barnes and Farmer were. A few seconds later, a red dot appeared on the screen registering the tracking device. After about a minute of calibrating, the GPS showed them going down the road, but the red dot was bleeping behind them.

"STOP!" Barnes shouted.

Frightened by his intense scream, the older man hit the brakes and slid to the side of the road.

"What are you screaming about?" asked Farmer. "You nearly scared me to death."

"They're behind us," said Barnes in an anxious voice. "I don't know how, but they are not in front of us like we thought they would be. The red dot is saying that they are a little over a mile behind us on this road."

Farmer put the car back in drive, made a U-turn, and started back down the road slowly following the directions of the device's GPS. They drove and then saw the dirt road off to the left and caught a glimpse of the back of the Jeep. The Jeep could not be seen from the direction they had come, but it was now down a dirt road in a parking area for fishermen. They stopped to watch, but the red dot was moving farther away.

"They're not here," said Barnes. "They're on the move in the swamp. How are we going to keep up with them there?"

"Maybe we can rent an airboat from Jungle Erv's back in Everglade City," said Farmer.

The two men pulled out of the parking area and headed back to the motel and then to Jungle Erv's. As soon as they parked the car, they went into the airboat company's office and arranged to rent an airboat. Jungle Erv gave them a map of the swamp, started the airboat, and took them on a quick demonstration ride showing them how to operate the vehicle. Farmer and Barnes knew they were losing time with the demonstration, but they had no choice; neither of them knew how to drive the airboat. Surprisingly, driving the airboat turned out to be more fun that they thought.

After dropping off Jungle Erv at the dock, they began to head in the general direction of the dot on their GPS using the map he had given them. Following Dr. Miller, the boys, and Nokosa-bear was not easy because Farmer and Barnes could not go in a straight line. Instead, they had to follow the fingers of the swamp. It was time consuming because the streams moved in all different directions, and there were a lot of dead ends. But they at least had the advantage of knowing where the backpack was because of the tracker. As Barnes checked the GPS again, he saw that the red dot was no longer moving, which gave the men a chance to catch up to them.

"Is this the place?" asked Dr. Miller as he stepped out of the boat.

Nokosa-bear had already fired his shotgun and waited to make certain the alligators were gone, something that surprised Dr. Miller but had become common to the boys. They did see one alligator leave an area far to the right of them but knew that it wouldn't be a problem because it was a good way from their destination. The boys walked over with their machetes in hand and cleared off the brush to reveal the wooden framework they had uncovered yesterday. In the meantime, Nokosa-bear had pulled the metal detector out of the boat and was setting it up.

"Boys, grab the shovels that are in the airboat," Nokosa-bear directed.

The old Seminole slipped on a headset attached to the metal detector, which made a beeping sound when it came across anything metal. He began to walk closer to the ship sweeping the round plate at the bottom of the pole that detected metal in a back-and-forth motion much like the boys had used to cut the brush and vines. He was still a few feet away from the framework when it began to make a low beeping sound.

"There is something metal under me," Nokosa-bear exclaimed.

"Even though this is a wooden boat, there is going to be a lot of metal pieces. Hopefully, something we dig up will have a name on it or a date," Dr. Miller said.

"Okay, boys, let's dig here," Nokosa-bear directed, and the teenagers took out their shovels and began to dig.

Whatever had set off the metal detector was not right on top but was a foot deep. It was the metal left on a sail block, the pulley that allows the sailors to control the sails with ropes or used to lift objects off of the deck. Juan set it on a clear plastic tarp that Nokosa-bear brought in the boat. The four of them had decided to place anything they dug up on the tarp, so it could be photographed and labeled.

Nokosa-bear continued his search and frequently came across beeps from the metal detector. Most were things like forks and other sundry items from the ship but none with names or markings to help them. They continued their search creating quite a collection of items on the tarp they had dug up. Most of the items were between one and two feet deep into the ground; hardly any were on top. Dr. Miller and the boys kept busy digging as Nokosa-bear kept marking spots that set off the detector.

All of a sudden, Dalton stopped in his tracks. He had that strange feeling again but knew that their deception should have placed the guys in Fort Myers by now. At the same time, he heard a noise back off in the distance, the same kind of noise that an airboat makes as it is flying through the swamp.

"Stop! Do you hear that?" asked Dalton.

Dr. Miller and Juan immediately stopped working. Given his headphones, all Nokosa-bear heard were the beeps from the detector. Dr. Miller grabbed Nokosa-bear's arm and lifted a finger to his lips to get his attention. Nokosa-bear stopped, looked at Dr. Miller, and took the earphones off. It took him a couple of seconds to adjust to not using earphones, but he quickly heard what Dalton had heard.

"It's another airboat," the Seminole said. "The swamp is large and sound can carry across the water, so it could be going any direction and quite a distance away, but we need to be cautious."

After waiting a few minutes, the four of them went back to work, except this time Dr. Miller kept an eye out for anyone who might be approaching them.

Nokosa-bear waved the wand in a path outlining the framework, and the beeping sound filled his ears. He had moved it around to get an idea of how large an area they had to dig out. Either way he swung the detector, it beeped. When he walked left, it continued to beep for another six feet. Then he went back to his starting place, and it beeped to the right for two more feet. Whatever was underneath him was large, so he directed the boys to dig at the ends and then he put down the detector and picked up a shovel himself and started in the middle. Juan had not gone six inches when his shovel struck something metal. A couple of minutes later, Dalton hit metal on his end. Both boys continued to dig toward each other, hitting metal the whole time. Nokosa-bear also hit metal after a few minutes, but instead of digging toward the boys, he dug across to see how wide the object was. After clearing an area sixteen inches across, he dug down to see how deep it went. The deeper he dug, the more he realized what he was digging up, but he didn't say anything.

The boys will figure it out in a few minutes and that will be more exciting for them, Nokosa-bear said to himself.

Dr. Miller had been watching his son and Juan dig and watching the water. He had retrieved the shotgun that Nokosa-bear had used to clear the alligators, feeling that if someone were after them, there would be no one to help them. He returned to the dig armed with his normal pistol and a shotgun, knowing that Nokosa-bear also kept a pistol on him in the swamp and the boys had their knives and machetes. They wouldn't be much use if they had to defend themselves, but hopefully enough if necessary.

As Dr. Miller walked back over the mound, he immediately saw the size and shape of what they were digging. Nokosa-bear stopped him from saying what it was by holding up his hand and shaking his head. He pointed at the boys and Dr. Miller understood. This was all about the boys; they needed to be the ones to make the finds so both the adults waited with smiles on their faces.

Dalton stopped shoveling for a minute and looked up. He saw how much area he had cleared and how much Juan had cleared and the cross-section where Nokosa-bear had dug. He looked with a quizzical look and shouted, "Juan, it's a cannon!"

Juan furrowed his eyebrows and then looked all around. "You're right. What else could be this long and this wide on a ship?" Their excitement grew as did the speed of their digging. Juan scraped away some dirt and found some writing on the metal face. He got down on his knees and brushed away the dirt with his hands. Immediately, everyone else stopped and went to his hole. Juan made out the letters in the rusted metal. Clearing the dirt out of the crevices, he spelled out *El Dorado*. A loud shout went up by all four of them. They had found the ship that Captain Antonio de Torres had written about in his journal, the lead Spanish ship that carried the governor and the gold.

Their cheers turned quiet when they heard the approaching airboat.

"Quick, move away from the boat back into the brush," Nokosa-bear ordered.

Dr. Miller, the boys, and Nokosa-bear carried their shovels away and hid. None of them could be clearly seen from the water, but their boat could be spotted since it was close to the shore. They waited, hoping it was just fishermen passing by.

As soon as Farmer and Barnes rounded the corner, they saw the beached airboat and immediately shut their engine down. They knew that there was not much chance of being quiet now, but they tried, pulling up to the shore thirty feet upriver from Nokosa-bear's boat. The two men from the motel slid in quietly as Nokosa-bear, Dr. Miller, and the boys watched in the distance. They were surprised they had been followed but not surprised that it was Farmer and Barnes. Dr. Miller motioned the rest of the group to move back farther and watch.

Back at the motel, Mr. Langston looked out his front window and saw the two men's car over at Jungle

Erv's. He immediately picked up the phone and called the airboat company owner.

"Hey, I see the car of the two men who are staying here at the motel over at your place. What are they doing?" he asked

"I rented them an airboat," Jungle Erv said. "They seemed anxious to go out in the swamp."

Mr. Langston explained to Jungle Erv what was going on, and he immediately began to panic.

"Sorry, I didn't know," said Jungle Erv.

Mr. Langston hung up the phone and called the sheriff and told him to come quickly. By the time Mr. Langston had walked over to Jungle Erv's Airboat Tours, Jungle Erv had turned on a tracking device he had in each of his airboats. In the past, he had had to go out searching for boats that had broken down, so he had tracking devices installed on each one, and it had saved him enough search time to pay for itself. Luckily, this airboat's device immediately came on and he was able to place it on the map.

Twenty minutes later, the sheriff arrived with his siren blaring and Jungle Erv motioned him into his personal airboat. As soon as Mr. Langston and the sheriff were buckled in, he stepped on the accelerator and turned the boat in the direction of the main river. He flew through the swamp as fast as he could and still remain safe. The good thing was that Jungle Erv was used to giving tours and going out into the swamp so he knew where he was going and could travel at a fast pace to get there. The three of them knew that they needed to hurry fearing what the two men would do if they found Dr. Miller, the teenage boys, and Nokosa-bear.

After slipping their boat up on the shore, James Farmer and Nick Barnes got out and started walking along the water's edge trying to sneak up on where they thought Dr. Miller and the boys were working. Nokosa-bear stepped out in the open with his shotgun and hollered at them.

"Don't move any closer, Farmer!" he shouted.

The two men stopped but doubted the Seminole would shoot, so Barnes slipped up into the reeds toward the land unseen and tried to approach Nokosa-bear from behind.

"You need to get back into your boat and leave. You need to check out of the motel and leave the area now," Nokosa-bear demanded.

"We can't do that. Our boss knows you are hunting for treasure and he wants the gold," Farmer called back.

"We don't know what you are talking about," shouted Nokosa-bear.

Farmer continued, "We know you found a barrel from 1502 and that you searched through the archives for weather and history at the University of Miami. You are looking for one of the caravels from 1502 that was lost in the hurricane carrying gold back to Spain."

Dr. Miller, the boys, and Nokosa-bear were astounded at how much information the two men knew about their find.

During the exchange, Barnes continued moving up to outflank Dr. Miller and the boys. He thought if he

could get behind them he would have them surround-
ed.

"Where's your partner?" Nokosa-bear called out.

But before Farmer could answer, they heard a loud
hissing sound. Juan and the Millers knew what that
sound was, and they turned to look toward the grass to
see its source. A shot rang out, and the younger man
came bursting through the reeds chased by a twelve-
foot alligator. Nokosa-bear tried to aim, but between
Barnes and Farmer he didn't have a clear shot. It was a
wild scene with a young man running and this
prehistoric-looking beast flailing its tail and pumping its
short legs in hot pursuit. It was obvious no one had
told Barnes about running from alligators because he
kept running in a zigzag pattern like he was trying to
keep from being shot, but all the while the reptile was
gaining on him. As he burst through a taller patch of
grass, the alligator caught him, dragging him into the
swamp water.

James Farmer began shooting at the animal, un-
loading fifteen shots into the water. Everyone watched
in pure horror as they saw Nick Barnes bob up to catch
his breath, wide-eyed and then screaming. Everyone
breathed a sigh of relief thinking that Farmer must have
hit the alligator and killed it. But when Barnes screamed
again and was furiously dragged back underwater
fighting for his life, everyone stood shocked. Their
emotions were running from fear, to relief, to horror as
they watched this nightmarish scene play out in front of
them. There was nothing anyone could do. A shot in
the water might hit Barnes. But if they did nothing, the
alligator would win.

Watching the water boil as the beast and its prey thrashed around in the murky water was frightening. Then abruptly the water calmed, but Barnes never came up. No one could take their eyes off of the spot or close their gaping mouths from the terror they had just witnessed.

In all the commotion, no one paid attention to the other airboat coming up quickly. Nokosa-bear looked up and immediately recognized who was in the boat and waved them over. He screamed for them to look for the young man and the gator in the water, but the search proved futile after a few minutes. Jungle Erv's airboat pulled up onshore and Jungle Erv, Mr. Langston, and the sheriff got out.

Completely outnumbered and having lost his partner, James Farmer was too numb to put up a fight so he surrendered to the sheriff. There was no hope of completing the mission for his employer, Mr. Lanning. The sheriff took the pistol Farmer had in his hand and sat him down in Jungle Erv's airboat. After questioning Farmer, the sheriff realized that Farmer was only possibly guilty of stalking and that would require Dr. Miller to press charges.

"Dr. Miller, do you wish to press charges against this man?" the sheriff asked.

It did not take Dr. Miller long to come up with an answer considering they had all just watched the gruesome death of Farmer's partner, Nick Barnes.

"No. He only scared us but didn't harm us," replied Dr. Miller.

In his confession, Farmer explained that he and Nick Barnes were always trolling social media for possible sightings of historical finds that would produce treasure. He explained that it was Barnes's programs and devices that were able to break into anything put out on the airways that allowed them to even find the Snapchat in the first place. The program happened to see Dalton's post, and then he went on to tell them that they had bribed people in places like the library at the University of Miami to keep them posted about anyone who was searching records that would be tied to treasure. Everything else they found by watching until finally they placed a tracking device in Juan's backpack that guided them to Dr. Miller's spot in the swamp.

Given the stalking and the shots fired, the sheriff handcuffed Farmer but allowed him to move around with the rest of the group as they walked back over to the area where the ship was buried.

Mr. Langston exclaimed, "I can't believe that you came down here hunting snails and found a ship that looks to be more than five hundred years old."

"To tell the truth, I wasn't the one who found the ship or any of the clues," said Dr. Miller. "It was the boys. They stumbled across the pieces of wood and did all of the research on what they found. They even came up with what to look for out in the swamp. I think Nokosa-bear would agree with me that we were just along to keep them safe and to do the things they could not do."

Nokosa-bear nodded his head in agreement.

"I just got to watch the boys and drive the boat. I may have scared an alligator or two, but I am from the swamp they are not," Nokosa-bear admitted.

Then everyone walked over to take a look at the wreck. They stared at the hull in amazement and peered down into the hole where the cannon lay with its inscription. None of them could have imagined being witness to anything like this in their lifetimes. For protection, Dr. Miller and Nokosa-bear had not discussed what was potentially in the ship. They felt it was best to keep it quiet until it could be recovered, even if the sheriff, Jungle Erv, and Mr. Langston had saved their lives. The boys had learned firsthand how something so simple as a tweet could cause problems.

After discussing how important security was for an archaeological site and how significant this find could be, Dr. Miller said he would contact Southern Methodist University. Given the discovery, he was confident the university would be interested in funding and doing the excavation. Each person agreed to keep the news to himself until SMU had taken over the project and had given their permission to talk about it.

As an added precaution, James Farmer agreed to remain at the motel without contacting anyone until the site had been secured. He did not want to risk having the sheriff charge him with any offenses. He was past the job phase and now was truly curious about what the boys had found.

Jungle Erv loaded the sheriff and James Farmer in his boat and headed back to the marina. Mr. Langston agreed to drive back Jungle Erv's other airboat. Nokosa-bear, Dr. Miller, and Dalton headed back to Dr. Miller's car and agreed to rendezvous at the motel in the Millers' room later that day. As soon as Dr. Miller had cell phone coverage, he called the university and spoke with the president, explaining what they had found and the possibilities the find had. The president quickly chased down the head of the archaeology department, Dr. Frances Weston, ordering her to drop what she was doing and make arrangements to go to Everglade City with the appropriate number of staff. Her second call was to Mr. Howard Swartz, head of security for the university, to make necessary arrangements to protect the site of *El Dorado*.

Dr. Weston then called Dr. Miller, who filled her in about all of the facts and details. She was amazed at the story and promised to be there as soon as possible, along with her team. She asked Dr. Miller to make arrangements for their accommodations at the motel.

Later at the motel, when everyone assembled in Dr. Miller's room …

"Here is what I know," Dr. Miller shared with the assembled group. "As of now, Southern Methodist University headed by Dr. Weston from the archaeology department will be in charge of the excavation of the site. Mr. Swartz has arranged for a company out of Miami to provide security for the dig, and they will arrive tomorrow to begin protecting the site. Dr. Weston arrives at the end of the week along with her team to start a proper excavation of *El Dorado*."

He then told the group that they could not return to the site or speak to anyone about their discovery. Security was crucial to keep the site from incurring any damage or looting. The university was supposed to fax paperwork for everyone to sign to pledge their silence. So, Mr. Langston left the meeting to check his office fax machine to see if the paperwork from SMU had arrived.

After everyone signed the paperwork, Nokosa-bear headed back to the marina and promised to bring the log to them the next day. Mr. Langston and Jungle Erv headed back to their offices, laughing about how they had lived their whole lives and never knew *El Dorado* was out in the swamp. James Farmer just took it all in. He was excited for the find but very saddened by the loss and tragic death of his partner.

Juan said to Farmer, "I don't know what your intentions were for us, but I want you to know that I forgive you and am very sorry and disturbed by the death of your partner. It was a horrible way to go and one I will never forget."

"Thank you," Farmer replied. "I never wanted to do anything but follow my boss's orders. I am sorry for the problems we caused you."

"To tell the truth," said Juan with a smile, "it made it more exciting for us to think we were being watched and trying to stay a step ahead of you."

Then he turned to the sheriff and asked, "Can you uncuff him if promises to not put up a fight?"

The sheriff turned to Farmer and said, "Can you do that?"

"Absolutely," Farmer replied, and the sheriff released his cuffs.

The sheriff left soon afterward warning Farmer that if he caused any trouble for them he would not hesitate to carry him off to jail. Farmer nodded in agreement, no longer the antagonist but now a spectator to one of the greatest finds in America.

Epilogue

The team from SMU arrived at the motel at the end of the week. They rented out most of the rooms at the motel, except for a couple of rooms that were reserved for those people who were regulars, which made Mr. Langston happy. Jungle Erv rented them airboats on extended contracts and even went out periodically to help haul things back to his warehouse, which the university also rented as a place to do their research. So, Jungle Erv was also happy. The boys were allowed to return daily and learned how to properly excavate a site. They enjoyed digging and marking finds the rest of the summer.

With a crew of ten people meticulously digging, they were able to reach the cargo holds of the ship. It had been crushed because of the rotting of the wood and the weather, but out of courtesy Dalton and Juan were the first to climb inside to see what they had found. There lashed to the bulkhead was a table of gold and chests of gold and other treasures. They took pictures and came back up showing all who were working what was inside. Only Dr. Weston, Dr. Miller, Nokosa-bear, Juan, and Dalton knew what the cargo manifest had read, so when they came out with pictures everyone was shocked. The two boys were beaming with pride and excitement about their find and about their summer vacation. Dr. Weston thought that it would take close to six months to completely excavate the ship and move it to a place to be studied. She promised that she would keep Dr. Miller and the boys informed about what was going on and she thanked them for getting her involved.

The boys returned home with tales to tell their friends, because once all of the gold and artifacts were safely removed and secured, everyone was free to talk about their adventures. Dr. Miller completed his research on the mate-selection process of snails while the boys were with the archaeology team. Nokosa-bear returned to the marina with a smile on his face about his great adventure.

What happened to the money? It was rightfully the property of the finders, the United States, and the original owner, Spain. The finders—Dr. Miller, Dalton, Juan, and Nokosa-bear—gave their finders' title to SMU to help the university finance the dig and secure the site. According to a 1902 treaty between the United States and Spain, Spain was the owner of the treasure. But it willingly paid a large finders' fee to SMU for their efforts to restore Spanish history and acknowledged Dr. Miller, Dalton, Juan, and Nokosa-bear for discovering *El Dorado*. Instead of accepting Spain's offer of several million dollars, Nokosa-bear agreed to a smaller settlement and bequeathed most of it to the Seminole Tribe of Florida Historical Preservation Office. Dr. Miller's research on snails would be fully funded at SMU for as long as he was on staff. The university paid for the boys to spend their last week of vacation at Disney World and then paid for them and their families to go to Spain when the *El Dorado* exhibition was on display in Madrid the following year. SMU also offered both boys full scholarships when they graduated from high school.

What the boys did not know was that Spain and SMU arranged to place $20 million in trusts for each boy. They were not to be told about it until Dalton's thirtieth birthday. This way, they would not be hounded for money and hopefully grow to be outstanding and responsible young men.

Over the next sixteen years, Dalton and Juan never really wanted for much. They just lived normal lives, dating, playing soccer, finishing school all the while continuing to be involved in historical adventures. Both boys took up the offer for scholarships at SMU and went on to earn degrees and begin careers and families. They never forgot that adventurous summer, but most of all they remained best friends.

Dr. and Mrs. Miller decided to throw Dalton a thirtieth birthday party at the Mansion Restaurant in Dallas. They invited Juan and all of his family to the event, and secretly invited the president of SMU and the head of the Historical Society of Spain. Dalton and Juan were surprised and honored when they realized who was included on the guest list. But their surprise turned into shock when the president and society head revealed the gift that had been waiting for them all these years—their trust funds.